WHAT OTHERS ARE SAYING—

"Crippled emotions are nothing new, but since 9/11, I have observed a whole new level of crippling fear, anxiety, restlessness, and depression. Something has slipped, badly jarred loose, in America and in the West. Dr. Mark Walker has just the antidote we need to quit losing at mind games we ought not play at all."

—Dr. Mark Rutland
President, Oral Roberts University

"It is the will of Christ that we have peace of mind and live committed, contented, and creative lives. The will of Satan is just the opposite; he wants to play mind games and fill our minds with thoughts that sabotage peace—confusion, conflict, crises. In *Mind Games*, Dr. Walker sets a positive path to deal with and overcome mind games such as discontentment, fear, and depression. His style is refreshing, intriguing, and faith-building. Your mind and life will be enriched and energized by the solid content of *Mind Games*."

—Raymond F. Culpepper, D.D.
General Overseer, Church of God

"Anyone desiring to be spiritually mature must read Mark Walker's powerful message of hope in his new book *Mind Games*. Expect to receive revelation and fresh insight into the Spirit-filled life. A must read!"

—Ann Platz
Author, Speaker, Interior Designer

"In *Mind Games* my friend Dr. Mark Walker not only leads us to understand the genesis and feeding of thoughts that threaten to cripple us, but he helps us to overcome them and live triumphantly—be a winner."

—Dr. Samuel R. Chand
www.samchand.com

"Every game has an opponent—sometimes it is one's self. Every winner has a strategy—it doesn't come accidentally. A winning strategy is consciously developed. It is calculated. It involves spiritual choices. Dr. Mark Walker recognizes universal pain and loss as part of the human condition. He skillfully lifts up the work of God through Christ Jesus as the ultimate plan. He offers the truth and necessity of the Bible as the consummate "play book." *Mind Games* will lead you to God and His Word; God and His Word will lead you to victory."

—Mary Ruth Stone, Ed. D.
Director of Faculty Development
Lee University
Cleveland, Tennessee

"If you are serious about living the abundant life, be careful what influences your thinking! The Enemy of your soul will seek access to your mind and create unnecessary hurdles to God's design for your joy and peace. *Mind Games* is an exceptional guide for the serious disciple of Christ and Dr. Mark Walker is a gifted communicator. His work here will help you navigate life's journey!"

—William E. Isaacs
Administrative Bishop
Church of God, Northern Ohio

"*Mind Games* is more than a book; it is a key that can unlock the prison of your mind. This book addresses some of the primary social and spiritual issues of our day. Dr. Mark Walker is passing along lessons that took a lifetime to learn. Some books inspire you to change, some books inform you so that you can change, but this book changes your paradigm, which changes everything. It's a must read."

—Bryan Cutshall, D.Min.
Senior Pastor
Twin Rivers Worship Center
St. Louis, Missouri

"*Mind Games* is a practical, sound, helpful, and insightful book for anyone or everyone. Dr. Mark Walker has so succinctly given the tools needed for good mental health and spiritual growth and development, written in an easy to grasp style with profound Truth. Most of us, at times in our lives, struggle with the mind games of belief, fear, discontentment, depression, and negative attitudes that he addresses. This book will challenge our thinking with truth and his humorous personal stories will encourage us to pursue the mind of Christ for healthier Christian living."

—Gail Clark Lemmert, M.A., NCC
Minister of Spiritual Formation
Westmore Church of God
Cleveland, Tennessee

"Get ready! You are about to encounter a powerful exploration of the battle of the mind. *Mind Games* provides ways to overcome crippling thoughts that threaten to control every facet of daily life. Straight from a pastor's heart, each page is filled with a distillation of practical insights founded upon the bedrock of Scripture. Mark's warm, personal style presents a rich mine of discovering Christ's hope and healing for healthier thinking. *Mind Games* is relevant, fresh, inspiring, and challenging. Without a doubt, it's food for your soul, your heart, your life—for your mind!"

—Michael L. Baker
Administrative Bishop
Church of God, Virginia

Cindy,
God bless you as you continue to
touch the lives of the born &
unborn.
Pastor Mark
Rom 12:2

MIND GAMES

OVERCOMING CRIPPLING
THOUGHTS THAT THREATEN
TO CONTROL OUR LIVES

MARK L. WALKER

MIND GAMES

OVERCOMING CRIPPLING THOUGHTS THAT THREATEN TO CONTROL OUR LIVES

FOREWORD BY PAUL L. WALKER

PATHWAY PRESS

Editorial Staff: James E. Cossey, Tom George, Tammy Hatfield, and Candice Branam-Snyder

Cover Design by Michael McDonald
Interior Design by Tom George

Library of Congress Control Number: 2009937632

ISBN: 9781596844841

Copyright © 2009 by Pathway Press
1080 Montgomery Avenue
Cleveland, Tennessee 37311

Visit *www.pathwaypress.org* for more information.

Printed in the United States of America

DEDICATION

Mind Games is dedicated to my
beautiful and wonderful wife, Udella.

I not only fell in love with your gorgeous looks,
but also your incredible mind. Your thinking is
healthier than most anyone I know—
including my own.

You are a constant support to me and, at the risk
of sounding rather corny, I have to say that
you truly are my inspiration.

Thanks for putting up with my ranting at times and
for never losing confidence in me when I was
losing it in myself. I've said this often,
but it's worth repeating—
I definitely married up.

I love you with my entire being.

I'm looking forward to our
book project together.

CONTENTS

ACKNOWLEDGMENTS

To Deborah Mack, Dr. Marcy Hardy, and Pastors Ed Stone, Jeremy Isaacs, and Brett Mayes: thanks for reading the working copies of the manuscript. Your feedback was invaluable and quite helpful in shaping the final outcome of this work. Thank you for your time and genuine interest in seeing this book come to pass.

To Pastor James Byrd, I'm grateful you constantly "pestered" me to write a book. Without your relentless encouragement and firmly gentle (and sometimes not so gentle) pushing, this project wouldn't have been accomplished. You are my forever friend and mentor for whom I have the upmost respect, love, and admiration.

To my brother-in-law, Udel Richardson, thanks for the initial formatting of the manuscript and preliminary ideas for the book cover. I appreciate your guidance throughout this process and your amazing gift of graphic design. Most of all, I appreciate your friendship.

To Whitney Till, your energy, time, effort, leadership, attention to detail, and vision are why this book exists. Thank you for keeping me on track, encouraging me, and handling so much of what is often referred to as "grunt work." Your contribution to the completion of this book cannot be measured adequately. Just please know that I am hugely grateful for you, your commitment to excellence, your loyalty, and your belief in this work.

FOREWORD

In the book, *Mind Games*, Dr. Mark Walker presents a much needed study of the importance of dealing with the threatening thoughts that control our lives, and he charts a course for developing the authentic Christian life as the process for moving in a positive direction for the fulfillment of a productive lifestyle.

Drawing from his background of growing up in a pastor's family, living in a parsonage and moving from a secular, professional career to pastoring a three thousand member church, he provides contemporary insight into dealing scripturally and healthily with such important life issues as belief, discontentment, fear, depression, and attitude.

Utilizing his training in counseling and gleaning from his Mount Paran North parish experience, he writes in a way that explores the pressures of contemporary life and offers practical principles for facing up to dysfunctional fallout through personal adjustment and reliance upon the power of God.

In his words, "We can be well educated, highly trained, naturally talented, fully qualified and experienced, but we will encounter life-storms that will exceed all of these. Our faith must rest in something that exceeds us, our abilities, and any potential life-storm."

In addition, he makes the case that "Christ is the faith

source . . . and when storms come they don't heighten our fear—they heighten our faith."

As his father, I can substantiate that his life reflects the essence of this book, and it is the kind of information that will not only provide an important resource for pastors, but it also offers every person a "go to" support plan for facing up to handling those times when life seems overwhelming.

—Paul L. Walker, Ph.D.
Director of Local Church Development
Church of God International Offices
Cleveland, Tennessee

Pastor Emeritus
Mount Paran Church of God
Atlanta, Georgia

INTRODUCTION
THE GAMES WE PLAY . . .

Games are played all over the world by people of all ages. Whether a game of tiddliwinks, marbles, chess, *Halo 3*, *Madden NFL*, badminton, football, or cricket, all cultures seem to enjoy some sort of game-playing. We even make up games like the game my wife and I play called "Are they dating or are they married?" We watch couples in a restaurant or mall and guess whether they're married or just dating. Of course, there's no way to win because we never ask the couples to find out their relationship status. It's still fun for us nonetheless (and yes, maybe a bit weird).

Of the more traditional games, I loved to play board games growing up. Monopoly, Risk, Life, Sorry, Scrabble, and Mouse Trap were some of my favorites. I even play them now when I get the opportunity.

Whatever the game, I believe we play because we enjoy the competition, fun, strategizing, laughter, and entertainment games provide. Games are great distractions from the stress and reality of the world. They allow us to escape daily pressure in a healthy way. But games eventually end and we have to place them back in the box and return to real life. Unfortunately, many people treat real life as if it's a game, confusing reality and fantasy.

When we sense that people are "playing games" with us, we believe they are being dishonest with us. We feel they are attempting to deceive, use, or manipulate us. They try to create a false reality, getting us to do things that will benefit them at our expense. We don't appreciate it when people play games with our lives.

Yet, we tend to play games with ourselves. Our own thinking can deceive and manipulate us, creating our own false reality that causes us to make unhealthy choices. Such games occur in our minds and they're called *mind games*.

Mind games are the false understandings we act on as truth. They are the often subtle, yet sometimes pronounced, immobilizing thoughts that frustrate our lives. Mind games are the unhealthy views we formulate in our psyche that lead us into less-than-functional living. They are self-deceptions that trick us into believing we're living full lives when we are actually living beneath the purpose for which we were designed. Mind games affect us all, but they can be defeated.

The purpose of this book, *Mind Games*, is to provide ways to help us overcome the crippling thoughts that threaten to control our lives. The book emphasizes that the primary way to overcome mind games is through the person and work of Jesus Christ. Christ claimed, "I am the way and the truth and the life" (John 14:6) and offers that truth to us. The path to whole and healed thinking is through the Maker of our minds. He even promises us a sound mind (2 Tim. 1:7), a renewed mind (Rom. 12:2), and the very mind of Christ (1 Cor. 2:16). Looking through the lens of the truths and promises of fascinating Bible stories, *Mind Games* seeks to lead us into discovering Christ's hope, healing, and power for healthier thinking and living.

INTRODUCTION

Mind Games explores five common thought issues: *beliefs*, *discontentment*, *fear*, *depression*, and *attitude*.

Chapter one examines the belief game process that is critical to how we think and, ultimately, to how we live. The belief game process is foundational for healthy and wholesome thinking. It's essential to helping us overcome any potential mind game.

Chapter two explores the discontentment game. In this chapter, we'll discover the secret to contented living. Often, discontentment drives us into choices that wreak havoc in our lives. Because we seem to have an incessant need to measure our worth, value, and significance by what others are and have, we tend to make life-impairing decisions. The discontentment game unpacks the secret of contentment available to everyone.

Fear is perhaps the most common and, some would argue, the most fatal mind game of all. Fear is a unique motivational factor that can both help and hinder us. The fear game in chapter three looks at one of the great miracle stories of Christ to help us overcome hindering fear. Together we'll learn how to have productive fear while resisting unproductive fear.

Depression... doesn't the word itself make you depressed? Chapter four leads us through not only the complexities and challenges of the depression game but also to our source of healing and hope. The Psalms are a tremendous resource of help in times of depression. The depression game chapter walks with the psalmist of Psalm 42 down the road of depression to victory.

Finally, chapter five is about the attitude game. You've heard it said that the way to win in real estate is "location, location, location." Well, the way to win in our thought lives is "attitude, attitude, attitude." In chapter five, we discuss how to maintain a good and godly attitude, especially in painful times. We take a candid look at the short Old Testament story of Ruth and Naomi to learn how to win at the attitude game.

I pray that the Lord will use this small book as a tool to help us all better think with His mind. My hope is that this short read will inspire, challenge, convict, and equip us to overcome any crippling mind games threatening to control us. I invite you to join me in learning to play only games that can be returned to the box, not with our own minds and lives. Enjoy reading *Mind Games*.

—Mark L. Walker, Ph.D.

THE BELIEF GAME

Therefore, I urge you, brothers, in view of God's mercy, to offer your bodies as living sacrifices, holy and pleasing to God—this is your spiritual act of worship. Do not conform any longer to the pattern of this world, but be transformed by the renewing of your mind. Then you will be able to test and approve what God's will is—his good, pleasing and perfect will (Rom. 12:1-2).

M y wife, Udella, and I had the opportunity to take a tour of missionary work in South Africa. During our time there, we were able to participate in a couple of game drives on a thirty-five thousand acre private game reserve. In essence, it's a fenced-in jungle. Wild animals live and roam in their own habitat, and guides drive you around in open-air vehicles to see them. The animals are not in cages. They are not from the circus. They are not tamed or trained. They are wild animals in their own environment and you drive within fifteen feet of them just to say, "Hello, how are you doing?"

One of the main attractions of the reserve is a male lion named Zero. He is the big deal—the king of that particular jungle. But Zero is a rare sighting because he is often in the deeper parts of the bush where the vehicles can't go. Surprisingly, on one of our drives, Zero was located off the main driving areas, but not too deep into the bush that the vehicles couldn't get to him. So, off we went to blaze our own trail to Zero.

When I say the main driving areas, I mean a literal beaten path. There is no asphalt—it's a dirt road, and you sometimes wonder whether it's a road at all. Just as we were getting comfortable with these driving conditions, we suddenly veered off the road into dense thickets. We had to duck to avoid being scratched by vines, thorns, and branches, several of which were poisonous. Our driver had to tell us which ones to avoid touching while at the same time steering away from and around ditches and stumps. We were avoiding all this danger and hoping to see an animal that could kill us. It was awesome!

My wife wasn't thinking that this was nearly as awesome as I was. As we were driving into the jungle, she was insisting to the driver that we were going the wrong way and needed to turn back. I, on the other hand, couldn't care less about poisonous branches or ditches or stumps. I wanted to see this lion. And to be honest, I was hoping to ride him. To me, this was Disney World. To Udella, it was *Jurassic Park*.

Suddenly as we cleared another round of limbs and thorns, there was Zero. He was huge! His son was with him, almost as large as Zero himself. Next to them was the carcass of a giraffe they had killed. Both lions had been feasting on their kill for four or five days and were like me after eating Thanksgiving dinner—they couldn't move. Since the lions were so full, the guides knew it was safe to get close to Zero and his son because they couldn't have eaten us if they tried.

When we finally reached Zero, we were only about sixty feet from him and he was on Udella's side of the vehicle. It was great! My wife got closer to me on that day than she had in our entire marriage. I was so excited about seeing Zero that I stood up to take pictures, which is strictly forbidden. The guides were yelling at me to sit down, but I didn't care—I wanted a picture of the beast. My wife was not pleased and was threatening divorce (even murder).

Here we were, two people having the same experience with two completely different emotional responses. Udella's was total terror. Mine was sheer excitement. For her, we were way too close. For me, we couldn't get close enough. She couldn't get out of there fast enough. I wanted to stay there all day and night.

How can two people having the same experience have two completely different emotional responses? Zero wasn't doing anything different to her or to me. He was just sitting there moaning and groaning because of his gluttony. Why such diverse responses to the same experience?

Could it be that what Udella believed about the situation and what I believed about it generated the different responses? I believed the driver when he said, "Zero is so full of giraffe that he isn't going to do anything to us." On the other hand, Udella believed, "This is a killer animal, and I don't care how much giraffe he has inside of him, there is probably room for a Udella in there as well."

When we face a situation it is not simply the situation that causes our emotional, psychological, and behavioral responses, but instead, it's what we choose to believe about the situation. My beliefs determine what I will feel and do in response to a circumstance. It is what I call the belief game.

We play the belief game when we tend to blame our life-condition on our situation alone without taking into consideration our choices and beliefs in the matter. When we fail to see our responsibility in the issue, we can live as blaming victims or bitter villains. I believe much of our emotional, psychological, and behavioral conditions are the results of what we choose to believe about our experiences.

I am in no way discounting the unfortunate conditions of those who suffer a mental illness or chemical imbalance that alters their ability to clearly understand and choose. I realize that some people are psychologically afflicted and unable to believe, choose, and think rationally. For such persons, the belief game may have limited application without the help of professional care or medication. I thank God for the help He has provided through these means and through His supernatural healing.

Neither am I attempting to trivialize the life-altering effects that severe tragedies and traumas can have on people's lives. Rape, abuse, abandonment, sudden loss, and other traumatic events can inflict great damage on one's emotional and mental life. No doubt, these can leave painful emotional and psychological scars that have long-term effects. However, healing for such experiences is possible. Understanding the belief game is a major way God brings healing. Yes, it can take some time and a great deal of hard work, but healing is possible—very possible.

To better help us understand how to win at the belief game, let's look at a very important process the apostle Paul describes in Romans 12:2.

THE BELIEF GAME PROCESS

The Book of Romans was a letter written by Paul to the followers of Christ in Rome, Italy. He was writing about the forgiveness of sins, the righteousness of Christ, the new nature in Christ, and the indwelling of the Holy Spirit that God provided them (and us) through His grace and mercy. In chapter 12, Paul seemed to be instructing Christ-followers on how to respond to what God has done through Christ. Paul wrote in verse 2, "Do not conform any longer to the pattern of this world, but be transformed by the renewing of your mind. Then you will be able to test and approve what God's will is—his good, pleasing and perfect will."

The Greek word for *transform* is where we get the English word *metamorphosis*, which means to have a complete change of form, structure, or substance.[1] It's the word we use to describe how a caterpillar changes into a butterfly. When you compare a caterpillar to a butterfly, they are completely different, but one comes from the other through a complete and total transformation.

The Greek tense Paul used for the word *transform* means "ongoing and continuous"—not just a single occurrence. We don't really like the word *process* in our lives and society. We like drive-through, instant access, and high-speed. We want change right now. However, God makes some changes immediately, but others He does over time. In regard to transformation, Paul is talking about something that happens over time, yet begins with something that occurs immediately. You might say the transformational process is an instantaneous process.

At first glance, the term "instantaneous process" makes no sense. *Instant* means something that happens immediately, while *process* means a series of changes over an extended period of time. How can something be both an immediate change and a series of changes over time?

When we choose to follow Christ by faith and repentance, we instantly are forgiven of our sins. We have a new nature—the very nature of Christ. We are indwelt by the Holy Spirit, have eternal life, are a part of the body of Christ (the Church), and have the mind of Christ (John 3:16; Rom. 8:9-17; 1 Cor. 2:9-16; 6:19-20; 2 Cor. 5:17, 21; 1 John 1:8-10.) We are a brand new person—instantly! And now begins the process of learning how to live by our new nature and identity in Christ and how to think with His mind.

When my son and daughter were born, they were born instantly with everything they needed to be human—all the necessary limbs, fingers, toes, and vital organs. Immediately, all parts were in place for them to be human, not just a baby human, but an adult one. But what had to happen? They had to grow, mature, and develop into what it meant to be an adult human. They had to go through the process of learning how to use what they were born with instantly. It was a process of time, and still is.

As I come to Christ, instantly I have everything I need in Him to think, be, and do as He wants me to. But it is a lifetime process of walking with Him that brings it to pass. The beauty of a relationship with Christ is that He is constantly developing me, maturing me, and growing me up in His nature and mind. He's doing the transformation.

But what does this process have to do with the belief

game? Everything! It is the way by which we win the belief game. The transformational process in Christ enables us to change. Any type of unhealthy or ungodly attitude, emotion, or action, based in our beliefs about our life situation can be transformed by Christ into healthier and godlier beliefs, leading to healthier and godlier thinking and living. Literally, He can transform our minds to think and believe like Him, so that we can respond appropriately to our life-situations.

How does this work? Great question. Let's continue by defining a few more terms and phrases Paul used in Romans 12:2.

FAULTY BELIEFS

One phrase that's critical to the belief game process is, "Do not conform any longer to the pattern of this world" (Rom. 12:2). *Conform* means "to be in fashion or style; to look the same as."[2] When we say someone is in fashion, we mean they are dressing according to what society accepts as being in style. Their wardrobe reflects what the general population says is fashionable. In essence, to be in fashion (conform) is to act like, look like, and keep up with everybody else.

The phrase "pattern of this world" is referring to the views, ideas, and philosophies of the times. The term *world* isn't speaking of the cosmos but of the influences of the culture.[3] In this context, it's the counter-scriptural views, ideologies, philosophies, and understandings of our society. The pattern of the world is how the culture of the age views, interprets, and does life contrary to the ways of God.

Putting this together, Paul's statement seems to be instructing us to be careful not to be in fashion with the values, ethics, morals, and philosophies acceptable in our culture that are unacceptable to God. We are to avoid the patterns of viewing, interpreting, and doing life in a way that is in style with our age but out of style with God. A major part of the belief game process Christ wants to bring about in our lives is for us to recognize the ungodly views of society we are allowing to influence our beliefs about life.

I call these beliefs *faulty beliefs*. Something *faulty* contains flaws that cause malfunctions.[4] Aligning our way of thinking with what is contrary to God forms beliefs that are flawed and will, over time, eventually break down. If what we choose to believe about a life-situation is faulty—not in agreement with God—then our response will bring about malfunctioning consequences.

A structure built on a faulty foundation will stand for a short while, but unless the foundation is repaired or rebuilt, it will crumble bringing the entire structure down. It's the same with the consequences formulated from our faulty belief choices. They will only satisfy and fulfill for a brief time, but soon, like a flawed foundation they will give way leaving us empty and dissatisfied.

Christ gave a great example of this in a story that is often referred to as the parable of the wise and foolish builders (Matt. 7:24-27). He told of two builders that built their homes on two different foundations—one built on a foundation of sand and the other on rock. When rainstorms and floods came, the house on the sand was flattened, but the house on the rock stood firm. The purpose of Christ's story was to show the difference between those who hear Christ's words yet disregard them, and those who not only hear His words but put them into practice.

Can you guess who the sand-builders were? Right—the

28

ones who disregarded Christ's teaching. They continued to conform to the pattern of this world. Another way to say it is that they did not align themselves with God's way of thinking and lived by faulty beliefs—a flawed foundation by which they made unhealthy response choices. As a result, they were not able to stand—they malfunctioned.

On the other hand, the rock-builders listened and applied Christ's instruction. They were no longer conforming to the world's patterns. They aligned themselves with God's way of thinking and lived by firm beliefs that established a sure foundation by which they were able to make healthy response choices and stand strong even in very stormy life-situations.

Both builders experienced the same rainstorm, so why the different results? What they chose to believe about the same circumstance was different, producing very different responses. One's beliefs were faulty; the other's were sure. One was winning the belief game; the other was losing.

Look at the way Udella and I experienced Zero. The expert guide told us we had nothing to fear because Zero was gorged with giraffe. If we chose not to believe him, we would have been like the sand-builder in Christ's story and our beliefs would have rested on a faulty foundation resulting in unnecessary fear and anxiety. However, if we chose to believe the guide, then we would have been like the rock-builder in Christ's parable and our beliefs would have rested on a firm foundation enabling us to experience joy and excitement.

Christ is the expert guide of our lives. His words are what we must build the foundations of our lives on. He must be the source shaping what we believe about what we experience. But how do we go from faulty to firm beliefs?

REPAIRING THE FAULTY FOUNDATION

A part of our responsibility in the belief game process seems to be the need to make a consistent and honest assessment of our beliefs. Are they faulty or firm? We might want to ask ourselves how we are allowing the non-God views of the culture and/or our family history to shape our beliefs about our circumstances. How is what's fashionable in the world's views but not God's affecting how we're justifying and rationalizing our beliefs and responses? In order to identify faulty beliefs, ask yourself, *Am I more in line with what the culture, my family, and/or I say are acceptable beliefs and behaviors, or am I more in line with what Christ says?*

Important to note is that this is more than a self-assessment. The Holy Spirit is vital to this process. The Holy Spirit is God who abides in and with followers of Christ (John 14:16-17). Christ said He wouldn't leave us alone but would send to His followers the Holy Spirit who would be our counselor to teach us and lead us into all truth (John 14:25; 16:13).

The Spirit reveals the thoughts of God to us. He enables us to think with the mind of Christ. "The Spirit searches all things, even the deep things of God . . . no one knows the thoughts of God except the Spirit of God. We have not received the spirit of the world, but the Spirit who is from God, that we may understand what God has freely given us . . . we have the mind of Christ" (1 Cor. 2:10-12,16). The phrase "spirit of the world" is the same as *pattern of this world* we saw in Romans—it refers to the non-God views, ideologies, philosophies, and understandings of our society. In Christ, we have the Holy Spirit who enables us to think according to God's ways, helping us overcome the ungodly influences of the culture. Suffice it to say that only in open cooperation with the Holy Spirit can we accurately and successfully assess our faulty beliefs.

But what do we do as we identify faulty beliefs? How is the faulty foundation repaired? At the risk of oversimplifying the matter, we replace the faulty belief with God's truth. Remember, the builder who built his house on the rock was one who put Christ's truths into practice. He was living in alignment with God's view. The way to repairing and rebuilding faulty beliefs is to replace them with firm ones.

In a statement, the belief game process is the process of identifying faulty beliefs and replacing them with the firm truths of God.

Perhaps I can illustrate the idea. Let's say that one of my faulty beliefs is that everybody has to accept me in order for me to feel of value and worth. I get rejected. Since I believe that I must be accepted by everybody to be somebody, how might I respond in my actions, attitudes, and emotions? Perhaps I'd respond with depression, hurt, anger, revenge, self-loathing, unhealthy people-pleasing behavior—consequences that will eventually malfunction because they come from a faulty foundation.

Through my painful response and the help of the Holy Spirit, I see that believing I must be accepted by everybody to be somebody is faulty. And I come to the understanding of God's truth that my ultimate worth, value, and significance is not found in the acceptance of others but in the acceptance of Jesus Christ. This replaces my faulty belief and becomes my new firm belief.

If I get rejected again, what might my response be through my new belief? Obviously, I am not going to like it. No one likes to be rejected and there will most likely be some hurt, anger, and disappointment. We are human after all, not robots. But through the firm belief of God's truth, I might be able to forgive the person who rejected me. I don't have to feel bad about myself. I don't have to go into depression and self-loathing. I might even be able to do good to that person and pray for that person. I may decide to worship God in the midst of my rejection and help others dealing with the same kind of faulty beliefs. I don't have to collapse into a broken, angry, vengeful victim. Instead, I can have godly, healthy, and wholesome responses.

I know this is a simplistic illustration, but I trust it helps to show how the belief game process can work. But even more so, I trust it shows our ability and responsibility to choose what we believe about our life-situations.

The truth is that I can choose to blame my life-situation for my unhealthy or painful consequences and remain stuck in the crippling emotional thoughts and actions associated with them, or I can choose to rebuild and live free. I can choose to build on the rock of God's truth. So, when the storm hits, the foundation holds. The house stands. Sure, when the storm subsides, the doors and windows may be somewhat weathered, the landscaping may be a bit disheveled, and a few shingles may be missing, but they are easy repairs. The structure, however, is stable. No rebuilding necessary. No malfunctions. All major supports are sound. All is well because I've chosen a firm foundation, not a faulty one.

Ultimately, this calls for us to be students of God's Word. The Holy Spirit applies God's truth to our minds that brings the transformation to our thinking. In 2 Corinthians 10:4-5 Paul said, "The weapons we fight with are not the weapons of the world. On the contrary, they have divine power to demolish strongholds. We demolish arguments and every pretension that sets itself up against the knowledge of God, and we take captive every thought to make it obedient to Christ." We can trust the Word of God and the Holy Spirit to bring our faulty beliefs down, replacing them with the liberating truth of God.

The key to winning the belief game is to know that it is a process that we must engage and never quit!

RELOAD AND PULL THE TRIGGER

I recall the day my dad taught me how to shoot a shotgun. I was seven or eight years old. We went quail hunting but before we could go on the hunt, I had to learn how to operate the shotgun. Dad took me out into an open field and handed me a sixteen-gauge double-barrel shotgun. He gave me a few instructions about how to hold the gun, how to aim, and about the recoil I could expect. Even after hearing Dad's instructions, I underestimated the shotgun's power. I pulled the trigger and the recoil's kick drove the butt of the shotgun into my shoulder, knocking me flat on my back.

Okay—I was done! My shoulder was screaming with pain, my right ear was roaring, I was lying on the cold, damp ground in a pile of leaves, and my head was pounding. As far as I was concerned, the quail could live another day. I was out of there. I started to cry and tried to hand the shotgun back to my dad, but he would have none of that.

He said, "No, Mark, you need to shoot it again."

"I don't want to shoot it again," I responded through my tears.

"Son, I know it scared you and you're hurt, but it won't last and you can do this. Don't quit now—I won't let you."

Dad handed me two more shells and I reloaded. Although my first impulse was to shoot him, I fought off the urge, aimed at the target, and pulled the trigger. I stumbled backwards, but I didn't fall down. I tried to hand Dad the gun again, but he refused and made me reload and shoot. I pulled the trigger but didn't stumble. Instead, I remained firm. I kept the gun this time and put my hand out for the next two shells. I reloaded and fired.

Dad and I repeated this process several times until I was totally comfortable and fearless with the sixteen-gauge. When it was over, my shoulder felt like it was no longer connected to my body, I couldn't hear anything out of my right ear, I was covered with leaves and twigs, my face was streaked with tears, and my head was pounding out of its skull, but I was standing in complete victory. I wasn't defeated. It was worth it because I had the time of my life that day. I won because my dad wouldn't let me quit. He knew that if I let failure or fear rob me from trying, I'd never succeed.

We have a heavenly Father who does everything He can to keep us from quitting. He loves us too much to let us give up. I encourage you with Paul's words in 2 Corinthians 4:8, "We are pressed on every side, but not crushed; perplexed, but not in despair; persecuted, but not abandoned; struck down, but not destroyed."

If you've been struck down, get up. If you did get up only to get struck down again, get up again. God is with you. He knows what you can take. He has another shell for you. Reload and pull the trigger—God has not counted you out!

CHAPTER TWO

THE DISCONTENT-MENT GAME

I rejoice greatly in the Lord that at last you have renewed your concern for me. Indeed, you have been concerned, but you had no opportunity to show it. I am not saying this because I am in need, for I have learned to be content whatever the circumstances. I know what it is to be in need, and I know what it is to have plenty. I have learned the secret of being content in any and every situation, whether well fed or hungry, whether living in plenty or in want. I can do everything through him who gives me strength (Phil. 4:10-13).

O ver the years, my family and I have enjoyed snow skiing, especially my dad. He used to take at least one ski trip every season and became an accomplished skier. He was so accomplished, that often he would venture off the main slope and cut through the woods or take jumps.

One particular day, we were skiing and he decided to go through the woods. Unfortunately, he lost control and hit a tree, breaking his ribs and collapsing a lung. The ski patrol placed him on a stretcher and, to his humiliation, had to ski him out of the woods and down the slopes to the clinic.

The next ski season, Dad, Mom, and I were in Jackson Hole, Wyoming. Mom wasn't feeling well one morning, so she decided not to ski with Dad and me. However, she made Dad promise that he would ski under control and do nothing to jeopardize his health. Dad promised.

As we were leaving the condo, Mom looked at me and said, "By the way, it's your responsibility to make sure he keeps his promise." Well, dealing with Dad is sometimes like trying to deal with a strong-willed two-year-old. All my life, Dad has pretty much always done whatever he wanted, whenever he wanted. To watch him is a lot like trying to herd cats.

It was a beautiful day and the snow was great. We had made three or four runs and were on another run when Dad, about twenty or thirty yards in front of me, suddenly veered hard to the left. I looked and he was headed for a ramp to jump. He hit the ramp and, while in midair, turned sideways completely parallel to the ground. The parallel position is not a good position for landing on one's feet.

Dad hit the mountain broadside and became a human snowball. I skied toward him passing his skis, poles, gloves, and goggles. I thought the man was going to be naked by the time I reached him. When I got to him, he looked like two ski boots sticking out of a huge snow mound. He was covered in snow—it was in his mouth, ears, nose, hair, and all down his clothes.

When I was able to dig him out I asked him, "Dad, are you okay?" He looked at me, and with God as my witness, the first words out of his mouth were, "Son, whatever you do, don't tell your mother!" The bone in his leg could have been sticking out but the first thing he still would've said would've been, "Don't tell your mother!" (By the way, I haven't told my mother, and I am writing this in the strictest of confidence.)

If we analyzed what drove my dad to do what he did, we might conclude that one reason was discontentment. Perhaps he wasn't content with being the skier he actually was and only skiing where he needed to ski. Maybe he felt he had to go beyond his limitations and capabilities of skiing. In doing so, perhaps Dad found himself in a place where his skiing ability was not good enough for him. He went beyond his abilities into something that brought pain and suffering into his life. One might say he went for more than was needed when everything he needed was already provided for him.

Now, I don't know if discontentment was the reason, but everyone of us can relate to what discontentment can do in our lives. Discontentment can drive us beyond our means and limitations only to get us into places we are not capable of handling emotionally, spiritually, or psychologically. Discontentment can cause us to neglect, ignore, and not enjoy everything that has been adequately and sufficiently supplied to us. Discontentment can rob us of all confidence and gratitude. With discontentment, we have a tendency to go for more when we already have more than enough.

If we're not careful, discontentment can lead us into attitudes and actions that bring great pain and suffering into our lives. The Bible calls these actions and attitudes sin. They dishonor God bringing us regret and hurt. In fact, the apostle Paul addressed this issue with his protégé, Timothy, in his first letter to him:

> But godliness with contentment is great gain. For we brought nothing into the world, and we can take nothing out of it. But if we have food and clothing, we will be content with that. People who want to get rich fall into temptation and a trap and into many foolish and harmful desires that plunge men into ruin and destruction. For the love of money is a root of all kinds of evil. Some people, eager for money, have wandered from the faith and pierced themselves with many griefs (1 Tim. 6:6-10).

The topics of Paul's instructions to Timothy were contentment and discontentment although he specifically addressed them in the context of having a love for money, being greedy, and seeking to get rich. Paul wasn't saying money and wealth are wrong, but if we desire them because of discontented greed, then ruin is not far behind. Obviously, discontentment takes forms other than greed, but all forms can ultimately lead to hardship.

BIBLICAL CONTENTMENT

Biblically speaking, *contentment* means "being fully satisfied, adequately supplied, and sufficiently prepared."[1] The purpose of Paul's letter to the Philippians was to encourage and instruct them. Paul also wrote about his source of biblical contentment. At the time of his writing, Paul was in prison because of his faith in Christ. Evidently, the Philippian people were concerned about Paul and wanted to help him with some type of care package. "I rejoice greatly in the Lord that at last you have renewed your concern for me. Indeed, you have been concerned, but you had no opportunity to show it" (Phil. 4:10).

When the opportunity to help him arose, they didn't hesitate with following through and Paul rejoiced. But he seemed to be rejoicing for something other than their commitment of generosity. "I am not saying this because I am in need, for I have learned to be content whatever the circumstances" (v. 11).

Paul apparently wasn't rejoicing just because he received their care package. I'm sure he appreciated it and was blessed by it, but he seemed to be implying that there was another source to his joy. He even stated that he wasn't in need because he had learned to be content whatever the circumstances.

What a declaration! Can we really say we've learned how to be content—fully satisfied, adequately supplied, and sufficiently prepared—no matter the circumstances? I know I can't. If we could learn what Paul learned about contentment, think about what that might mean in our lives. How would our attitudes, actions, thoughts, reactions, intentions, and outlook towards ourselves, others, and life change? If we could truly be content more than not, we can only imagine how our lives would vastly improve—less worry, fear, anxiety, and dissatisfaction, and more peace, enjoyment, gratitude, and fulfillment.

Paul continued in his letter to expand on what he'd learned about contentment: "I know what it is to be in need, and I know what it is to have plenty. I have learned the secret of being content in any and every situation, whether well fed or hungry, whether living in plenty or in want" (v. 12).

Whether in plenty or lack, hungry or full, needs met or unmet, Paul was fully satisfied, adequately supplied, and sufficiently prepared. But what was the secret Paul discovered?

Before we go there, let's keep in mind that Paul was writing this letter from prison because of his faith in God. He was being unjustly treated, yet declaring that he was content. In fact, several times in his short letter Paul used the word *joy* or some form of it. How can someone in that kind of situation write about joy? Is it because he learned the secret of being content?

Even more amazing to me is that Paul appeared to be rejoicing not because he had received something from the Philippians, but because of what they were going to receive in return for blessing him.

> Not that I am looking for a gift, but I am looking for what may be credited to your account. I have received full payment and even more; I am amply supplied, now that I have received from Epaphroditus the gifts you sent. They are a fragrant offering, an acceptable sacrifice, pleasing to God. And my God will meet all your needs according to his glorious riches in Christ Jesus (vv. 17-19).

Paul seemed to be rejoicing over how God would reward them for their generosity. He wasn't as happy for himself as he was for them. How many of us, when in a really discontented state, rejoice when somebody else gets blessed? I tend to get jealous and angry soon followed by griping and complaining with self-pity and depression not far behind. And, I'm not in prison.

As I read Paul's words, I started thinking about the jealousy, greed, envy, selfishness, bitterness, resentment, lust, rage, lying, cheating, stealing, complaining, and depression bred by discontentment. My list isn't exhaustive, but I believe it contains some of the more common qualities of discontentment. Yet, Paul doesn't seem to have any of these issues. Why? What enabled a man like Paul, who was being unfairly treated and unjustly imprisoned, to write a letter about being joyful even when good things were happening to others? Could it be the secret?

HEALTHY AND UNHEALTHY DISCONTENTMENT

Before learning Paul's secret, I think some clarification might be in order. You might be wondering if biblical contentment means I won't have painful disappointments or that I shouldn't have any dreams, goals, or ambitions or that I shouldn't look to improve myself or strive for excellence. It almost seems that biblical contentment—being fully satisfied, adequately supplied, and sufficiently prepared—requires that I accept where I am and do nothing to change or better the situation or me. Perhaps we can better understand biblical contentment by understanding the difference between what I call healthy discontentment and unhealthy discontentment.

Healthy discontentment is not settling for less than one's best to honor God. It is not being satisfied with mediocrity because God isn't mediocre. I don't want to be content with a life that is less than its best in honoring God. Healthy discontented people want every aspect of their lives—relationships, work, finances, home, thought lives, ambitions, dreams, and accomplishments—operating at optimal levels for honoring God. Healthy discontented people desire to be fully satisfied, adequately supplied, and sufficiently prepared to honor God at, and with, their best.

Paul seemed to have a healthy discontentment. In fact, he wrote about it in this same letter to the Philippians. In chapter 3, Paul described his religious, educational, and family background that qualified him to be a better Jew than most (vv. 1-6). Yet we know his pedigree left him discontent, because Paul clearly stated that none of that mattered compared to knowing Jesus Christ (vv. 7-8). He even stated his life's purpose was to know Christ in both His resurrection and suffering (vv. 10-11). Then Paul expressed his healthy discontentment:

> Not that I have already obtained all this, or have already been made perfect, but I press on to take hold of that for which Christ Jesus took hold of me. Brothers, I do not consider myself yet to have taken hold of it. But one thing I do: Forgetting what is behind and straining toward what is ahead, I press on toward the goal to win the prize for which God has called me heavenward in Christ Jesus (vv. 12-14).

He wasn't settling for anything in his life that wasn't reflecting his desire to honor and know Christ—a healthy discontentment.

In other words, the measure of Paul's healthy discontentment was Christ. He measured who he needed to be, what he needed to have, and where he needed to go based on Christ. One could say Paul's life was shaped by the vertical relationship he had in Christ.

Unhealthy discontentment is being dissatisfied or ungrateful for what one has or where one is because someone else has more or is better off. In other words, you might say unhealthy discontentment is measuring whether or not I am fully satisfied, adequately supplied, and sufficiently prepared by who others are and by what others have. The problem is that when I measure my worth and value based on the "who" and the "what," I will remain in a perpetual state of discontentment because there is always somebody that has more and is better off. Unhealthy discontented people don't orchestrate their lives around what honors God, but around the status of others.

Sometimes, I think of King Solomon of Israel when I think of unhealthy discontentment. Solomon was the son of King David and Bathsheba. He was considered the wisest and wealthiest man in the world during his rule as king. Yet, this wise, wealthy man struggled with unhealthy discontentment. In his writings in the Old Testament book, Ecclesiastes, Solomon described his struggle. He enjoyed all kinds of pleasures, engaged in huge building projects, amassed large amounts of slaves, gold, silver, livestock, and wives, and by his own estimation, became far greater than anyone in Jerusalem's history (2:1-9). He summarized this time in his life with these words:

> I denied myself nothing my eyes desired; I refused my heart no pleasure. My heart took delight in all my work, and this was the reward for all my labor. Yet when I surveyed all that my hands had done and what I had toiled to achieve, everything was meaningless, a chasing after the wind; nothing was gained under the sun (vv. 10-11).

All Solomon's status and stuff left him *meaningless*, which in Hebrew means "worthless, empty, and futile."[2] This sounds quite the opposite from fully satisfied, adequately supplied, and sufficiently prepared. At one point Solomon said, "I hated life" (v. 17).

Solomon appeared to be measuring his contentment by the horizontal—by how much more than others he could possess. Even after he believed he had acquired more wealth and had become more famous than anyone Jerusalem had ever seen, Solomon still was unsatisfied. He seemed to have forgotten that his wealth and wisdom were not the results of his efforts, but the blessings of God (the vertical). Instead of investing himself in honoring God with all God had bestowed, Solomon was trying to outdo everyone around him. He wasn't satisfied with what God had provided and where God had him. The result was meaninglessness—an unhealthy discontentment.

The most important human being in my life is my wife, Udella. I love her with all of my heart. I can't imagine my life without her. She is my best friend. The next two most important human beings are our two wonderful children, Justin and Ashten. I love them more than life itself.

I have a wonderful job as a pastor. I love our church. Preaching to the people of our congregation is an awesome privilege. They pay me well to be their pastor. I am a blessed man!

My wife, children, and job are horizontal contentment sources, but they are not to be my primary contentment source. Do they add to it? Absolutely. Can they take away from it? Absolutely. But they weren't designed to be my primary resource of the full satisfaction, adequate supply, and sufficient preparation I need for the life God has available for me. As close to perfection as my wife is, as grand as my children are, and as wonderful as my job is, they will always fall short of bringing me total contentment. The horizontal always falls short, because it wasn't designed to be the ultimate source. That's why I can never be biblically content while being focused on who others are and what others have.

Paul couldn't, Solomon couldn't, and we can't. In fact, Solomon discovered that he had to shift from horizontal measures of contentment to the vertical measure. At the end of his attempt to fulfill himself with what he thought mattered, Solomon finally saw the light. "Now all has been heard; here is the conclusion of the matter: Fear God and keep his commandments, for this is the whole duty of man" (12:13). That brings us to Paul's secret. I think you probably know it by now.

THE SECRET

Returning to the words of Paul in Philippians 4, we see him writing about measuring his contentment by the vertical. He stated that he knew what it meant to be in plenty and to be in want; to be hungry and to be well fed; to be in need and to be fulfilled. Yet, he claimed that the good times of fulfillment and plenty were not the source of his contentment, and that the difficult times of lack and need did not rob him of his contentment. In other words, the horizontal was not going to determine or disturb his contentment.

Why? Could it be that he learned the secret?

> I have learned the secret of being content in any and every situation, whether well fed or hungry, whether living in plenty or in want. I can do everything through him who gives me strength (vv. 12-13).

Paul's secret was this: the full satisfaction, adequate supply, and sufficient preparation for life are found in Jesus Christ. Contentment was discovered in the vertical relationship available to him in Christ. Paul learned that through the times he had more than enough and through the times he had less than enough, Christ was his satisfaction, supply, and sufficiency. The horizontal couldn't provide the same contentment that Christ provided, nor could it deplete it.

Paul's discovered secret was that whether he had or didn't have in the horizontal, he always had what he needed in the vertical—Jesus Christ.

THE CONTENTMENT SHIFT

This calls for you and me to shift our primary source of contentment from the horizontal to the vertical—to live in the secret that Christ is our contentment. Here are three recommended shifts to live by:

Shift from who I am to whose I am. Focusing on who I am is focusing on me. It's solely depending on my intellect, abilities, talents, and insights to provide contentment's full satisfaction, adequate supply, and sufficient preparation. No doubt, God made us with incredible abilities, but for those to be used properly and efficiently, they must be surrendered to Him. They must be dedicated to honoring Him, which happens as I focus more on *whose* I am and less on *who* I am. I have to keep asking myself, *To whom do I belong, me or Him?* The only one of those two that is going to ever fully satisfy is Him.

Shift from what I have to who I have. Sometimes I will have enough in the horizontal, but there are other times when I won't. I need to realize that "what I have" in the horizontal can quickly become "what I don't have." At the time of writing this book, America is experiencing one of the greatest economic crises in our history. Many people have lost nearly their entire life-savings and retirement portfolios. Discontentment rages throughout the land. If a nation of people ever needed to know the secret of the true source of contentment, it's America. We've become very much aware that "what I have" can quickly become "what I don't have."

Paul is saying Christ never becomes a have-not. He never runs out. Christ is to be our full satisfaction, adequate supply, and sufficient preparation regardless of what we have or don't have. He is the ultimate possession for living.

Shift from where I am to where He wants me. Some of us may not be content where we are right now. But if we searched our hearts, would we say, "This is exactly where God has me"? If so, and we're not content, perhaps we need to pray, "God, You have me here. I believe that. Help me to embrace Your will for me. Help me to start rejoicing—to start finding joy. I want to be where You want me to be and I want to be content there. Be my full satisfaction, adequate supply, and sufficient preparation."

On the other hand, if we know where we are right now is not where God wants us to be, we need to move. Contentment will never be ours if we're not where God wants us—it's that simple. Obedience is a must for biblical contentment.

When my dad decided to veer off the main ski slope to take a jump, he was breaking his promise to my mom. He was not skiing within the limits placed on him by someone who knew what was best for him. Not to mention, he agreed to the limits. It wasn't when the jump went bad that he went wrong, but when he made the decision to break his promise. His decision to go another way put him in a place where he didn't need to be.

When we decide to usurp God's leadership for our lives, we head into places we don't need to be. He knows what's best for us. His limitations on us are for our good, not our detriment. If we are uncertain as to whether or not we're where He wants us, then I suggest getting alone and quiet with Him. Sometimes, we're so into our lives, we don't stop to listen to Him. If we've strayed, we'll know very shortly. God will reveal where we started veering off course. If so, let's shift from where we are to where He wants us. Let's repent and get back to where we know He wants us to be.

The lyrics to the song, "The Strength of the Lord," capture for me the essence of the challenge and answer to the contented life.

> Sometimes life seems like words and music that can't quite become a song. So we cry inside, and we try it again and I wonder what could be wrong.
>
> But, when we turn to the Lord at the end of ourselves like we've done a time or two before, we find His truth is the same as it has always been. We'll never need more.
>
> He's all we need for our every need. We never need be alone. Still, He'll let us go if we choose to live life on our own.
>
> Then the only good that will ever be said of the pains we find ourselves in, there are places to gain, the wisdom to say, I'll never leave Him again.
>
> It's not in trying but in trusting. It's not in running but in resting. It's not in wondering but in praying that we find the strength of the Lord.[3]

Let's learn the secret: "I can do everything through him who gives me strength" (Phil. 4:13).

CHAPTER THREE

THE FEAR GAME

That day when evening came, he said to his disciples, "Let us go over to the other side." Leaving the crowd behind, they took him along, just as he was, in the boat. There were also other boats with him. A furious squall came up, and the waves broke over the boat, so that it was nearly swamped. Jesus was in the stern, sleeping on a cushion. The disciples woke him and said to him, "Teacher, don't you care if we drown?" He got up, rebuked the wind and said to the waves, "Quiet! Be still!" Then the wind died down and it was completely calm. He said to his disciples, "Why are you so afraid? Do you still have no faith?" They were terrified and asked each other, "Who is this? Even the wind and the waves obey him!" (Mark 4:35-41).

When my son Justin was fifteen years old, he was not feeling well one night and couldn't sleep. So he came to our bedroom about two o'clock in the morning to ask if there was anything he could take to make him feel better. It was a cold night and he had a blanket wrapped around him all the way over his head like a hooded cloak. He came over to his mom's side of the bed but did not turn on any lights. In an effort not to startle her, he quietly bent over her to whisper in her ear. However, as he was bending over, Udella sensed this presence hovering above her and she opened her eyes. She saw this dark, silhouetted, hooded figure moving toward her face and she screamed!

Out of a dead sleep, I sat straight up in the bed and started screaming, but I had no idea what I was screaming at or about. Justin fell flat on his back, which sent the blanket flying in the air. He yelled back at his mom, "Mom, it's me, Justin!"

Meanwhile, still half asleep, I incoherently shouted, "Who? What? Where?"

Udella just screamed.

At two o'clock in the morning, my son, my wife, and I were shouting, yelling, and screaming at—well—nothing. For about thirty seconds, we were experiencing sheer terror when there wasn't anything terrorizing us. We were reacting to perceived fear.

Fear is an amazing animal. Perhaps there is no other emotional or psychological experience that has a more dynamic influence in our lives. On the one hand, fear can save our lives. On the other hand, fear has the potential to destroy our lives.

Psychologists tell us that fear is one of the first emotions we feel as infants. Fear is a natural lifelong experience. So, avoiding fear is not so much the issue as learning how to properly handle it. It's what I call dealing with the fear game.

FEAR—HEALTHY AND UNHEALTHY

The word *fear* has several meanings. It can mean to have an unpleasant feeling of anxiety aroused by impending danger, real or imagined; to be cowardly and timid; to have concern, anxiety, and nervousness; or to show reverence, respect, and awe.[1]

We can see by these definitions that fear can be healthy and unhealthy. *Healthy fear* is a rational understanding and response to a real threat, not a perceived threat, like your son with a blanket on his head peering over your wife. When we face a real threat and respond with an appropriate response to the danger of that threat, we have healthy fear. You've heard it said that the punishment needs to fit the crime. Well, healthy fear is the right amount of fear fitting the threat.

A healthy fear response heightens one's senses and abilities to optimum levels of effectiveness. It raises our mental, physical, and decision-making capacities to their most productive levels, allowing us the ability to handle our threat with sound judgment and rational thinking. Through healthy fear, we are able to make the best out of our fear-invoking threat.

Unhealthy fear is a free-floating or irrational fear from an unknown source. It may be fear issues that have accumulated in our lives over the course of time, which cause us to experience a constant sense of distress, anxiety, and nervousness, but we can't directly identify the real cause. It's just there. Unhealthy free-floating fear is living in a state of worry and anxiety without knowing why.

Irrational fear is another form of unhealthy fear. This is when we react inappropriately to a real threat or remain fearful of a perceived threat even after we realize that the threat does not exist. In other words, the punishment isn't fitting the crime—the fear level isn't fitting the threat level.

Such unhealthy fear responses can leave us paralyzed, withdrawn, or even in a sustained state of anxious dread. Or, we might find ourselves lashing out, obsessively controlling, or becoming overly aggressive. We can become immobilized emotionally, psychologically, and spiritually. If we're not careful, unhealthy fear can lead us into unproductive and damaging decisions and lifestyles.

In Mark's account of Christ calming a storm on the Sea of Galilee, he records how Christ dealt with the unhealthy fear that arose in His followers.

FEAR AND FAITH

The Sea of Galilee is a freshwater lake that is approximately eight miles wide and thirteen miles long located below sea level and surrounded by the hills of northern Israel. Because the lake has always teemed with fish and has been such a major water source for Israel, its region has always been a highly populated area, especially at the time of Christ. The way the lake is positioned beneath the surrounding hills, a sudden shift in wind can literally create a wind-tunnel effect that can bring on violent storms quickly and without warning. In Mark's story, such a storm seems to have blown in as Christ and His followers headed across the lake.

Jesus Christ was asleep in the boat as the storm raged and the disciples awakened Him to inform Him of their dilemma. Christ performed a miracle of all miracles by calming the wind, waves, and rain with a single word. He then asked two peculiar questions, "Why are you so afraid? Do you still have no faith?" (Mark 4:40).

Christ's questions used to bother me greatly because He seemed to be coming down on these guys for reacting in a very human way to such a life-threatening situation. Anyone that cared about life would be afraid in this type of a storm. I always felt Christ's questions were insensitive to His followers and out of touch with human reality. It was as if Christ was implying that we should never be afraid even in highly fearful circumstances. He just seemed unreal. But then I looked closer at what He asked.

Christ didn't ask, "Why are you afraid?" He asked "Why are you *so* afraid?" (italics for emphasis). Christ wasn't questioning their fear itself, but the level of their fear. He was asking, "Why has your fear level reached this height?" His question suggested that their fear was not fitting the threat. They were overreacting—they were having an unhealthy fear response.

But here's what's interesting to me, Christ didn't compare their level of fear to the magnitude of the storm. His fear measurement wasn't the threat of the storm; it was their faith!

Let that sink in a moment . . .

His fear measurement wasn't the threat of the storm; it was their faith.

Christ didn't downplay the size of the storm. His next words weren't, "This storm isn't that bad. You shouldn't be that afraid." He wasn't in denial. He seemed to realize that this was a whopper of a storm, one that would produce life-threatening fear. He knew what was going on.

Christ's next statement was another question about faith: "Do you still have no faith?" He appeared to be connecting their level of fear to their apparent lack of faith. It's as if Christ was saying that their fear-size was not the result

of the storm-size but the result of their faith-size. Their unhealthy fear wasn't a storm issue, but a faith issue. When
we place Christ's two questions together, He seemed to be
saying to the disciples, "Your fear has reached such a level
that you're reacting as if you have no faith."

All people believe in something—we all have faith. We
each have some type of belief system. We disregard that belief system for two reasons: we either don't trust in a source
that can handle all of life's storms or, we don't believe what
we are trusting in is capable of handling life's storms. Unhealthy fear arises when we don't believe in a sustaining
source or we don't believe that what we are trusting in can
sustain us. Our faith is either lacking or misplaced.

The obvious question then becomes, "In what can I place
my faith in order to have healthy fear responses?" Asking it another way, "How do I respond to fear-invoking circumstances
as one who has properly placed faith?" Using Mark's account,
let's first look at three fear and faith observations and then
examine how we might be able to shift from fear to faith.

FEAR AND FAITH OBSERVATIONS

Observation One: The object of my faith must be greater
than the size of my storm.

Most of Christ's followers accompanying Him across the
Sea of Galilee grew up on this sea. They knew how quickly
violent storms could come. But this storm was larger than
their training, experience, and expertise. It was beyond
their capability and confidence to handle.

We can be well educated, highly trained, naturally talented, fully qualified, and experienced, but we will encounter
life-storms that will exceed all these. Our faith must rest in
something that exceeds us, our abilities, and any potential

life-storm. Life is much like crossing the Sea of Galilee. We don't know when a sudden storm that is larger than we can handle will blow into our lives. Unless our faith rests in something that is larger than us and all of our life-storms, we will be like the disciples—responding with unhealthy fear that will lead to unhealthy living.

Christ is that faith source. He was attempting to show His disciples that He needed to be the object of their faith. He wanted them to place their trust in Him. By calming the storm, He proved with a single word that He was larger than any life-storm.

My family experienced the sudden wind of change when, in 1980, my older brother and only sibling, Paul Dana Walker, was killed in a head-on collision two days after Thanksgiving. As a family of pastors and ministers, we had counseled, taught, and preached to people that they can trust Christ in such painful and challenging times. We were highly trained and experienced in spiritual and faith matters. But our life-storm was greater than our training and skill. The Jesus who we talked about believing in had to become the Jesus we fully trusted. Our sermons and lessons weren't enough; we needed Him alive and real.

He didn't disappoint—just as He proved Himself as the storm-calmer to His followers that day on the sea, He proved the same to our family. We discovered that He can be trusted and that He is larger than any life-storm.

So, here's the question: "Where is the object of your faith?" Better yet, "Who is the object of your faith?" Is your faith-object greater than your storm?

Observation Two: Faith in Christ leads to more than temporary solutions to temporary problems—it leads to an eternal life plan for an eternal destiny.

Christ was asleep in the boat even after the storm hit and did not wake up until His disciples woke Him up crying out for help. Even though it appears that the fear of Christ's disciples overshadowed their faith, they at least knew where to turn for help. However, the tendency for many people is to call on Christ only when they have a problem.

Until they have a storm they can't handle, they want Christ to stay asleep in the boat and let them steer their own lives. When the storm strikes, however, they want Christ to wake up, bail them out of their problem, and then go back to sleep until they need Him again. They don't want Him to lead their lives as their Lord—they only want Him as a personal genie to help them out at their every beck and call.

Christ is, wants to be, and needs to be much more than a personal genie in our lives. He is, needs to be, and wants to be the Lord and Leader who provides us eternal, abundant life. He came so that we ". . . may have life, and have it to the full" (John 10:10). Christ promises that if we believe in Him we will have eternal life (3:16; 11:25). He offers us the best possible life now and forever. He doesn't want to be a passenger in the boat; He wants to be Owner and Captain.

Christ is to lead everything about our lives. When He is the leader who determines, defines, and directs our lives, storms don't heighten our fear—they heighten our faith. Even when death approaches, fear won't be allowed to rule because if Christ is our leader, His eternal life will rule.

One of my most memorable experiences as a minister was when I spent some time visiting a man who had been fighting terminal cancer. He had just received word from the doctors that they could do nothing else for him. Barring a miracle, he would soon die. I was trying to comfort him, but he ended up comforting me. My friend said, "Pastor, Christ is my life and should He heal me, I will spend the remainder of my days glorifying Him by telling of His great love and power. If He chooses for me to remain ill for a longer period of time, I will glorify Him until my death testifying of His sustaining comfort and grace. If He chooses for me to die soon, I will be with Him forever and my death will glorify Him telling of His eternal life. No matter what, Pastor, I can't lose!"

Christ wants to be more than a temporary solution to our problems; He wants to be our eternal source of abundant life.

Observation Three: Fear sees the temporary ruling the eternal. Faith sees the eternal ruling the temporary.

Although the disciples seemed to focus only on the storm, it was temporary and would soon blow over. It wasn't forever. What they were unable to focus on was the Eternal God of all creation in their boat. They believed the temporary storm was greater than the Eternal Creator.

Fear tends to take the temporal and exalt it above the eternal so that we begin to believe that the temporal life-storm is greater than the eternal resources we have in God. Faith looks past the temporal storm to the Eternal God who is greater than the storm.

In 2 Corinthians 4:16-18, the apostle Paul captured the tension that exists between living in the reality of temporal influences while desiring to live by eternal values. The Corinthian church was going through some difficult storms and Paul was trying to encourage and instruct them on how to deal with the storms from the eternal perspective. In these verses, he breaks down temporal and eternal: "Therefore we do not lose heart" (Fear can cause us to lose heart and hope.) "Though outwardly we are wasting away," (Our physical bodies are temporal and decay everyday.) "yet, inwardly we are being renewed day by day." (Our spiritual being is eternal and is made stronger daily in Christ.) "For our light and momentary troubles" (Troubles are temporary.) "are achieving for us an eternal glory that far outweighs them all."

According to Paul, our earthly troubles (storms) are temporary and light compared to the eternal existence that awaits us in Christ. And Paul seemed to be suggesting that our temporary life-storms actually work for us a better eternal life-experience. We can't beat the deal.

Paul concluded with the key to living in the temporary by the eternal, "So, we fix our eyes not on what is seen, but on what is unseen. For what is seen is temporary, but what is unseen is eternal" (v. 18). Listen to what he *didn't* say. Paul did not advise us to turn away from the problem as if to live in a state of denial. Jesus looked at the storm. It existed and He looked at it. Paul didn't instruct us not to look at our storm; he instructed us not to become fixated by it.

To become fixated by something is to become consumed and obsessed by it. We are not to let the storm consume us; instead, we are to become fixated, consumed, and obsessed with the eternal person, purpose, and promises of God. When the storm is pressing in, we know it's there and what its threat contains, but we choose to give our hearts, minds, emotions, and reactions to God. He steers us by His eternal purposes and power. Faith fixates on the Storm-Calmer; fear fixates on the storm.

So then, how do we shift from living less by fear and more by faith?

SHIFTING FROM FEAR TO FAITH

Rest in the One who is leading. "That day when evening came, he said to his disciples, 'Let us go over to the other side'" (Mark 4:35).

Who was leading this convoy? Christ. He initiated the trip across the lake. And where did He say they were going? To the other side. He didn't say, "Hey guys, let's go out in the middle, capsize in a storm, drown, and die." He said, "Let's go to the other side." Christ's promises will come to pass and no storm can stop them.

Did Jesus know they were going to run into a storm? Not really understanding how Christ exists both as one-hundred percent God and one-hundred percent man, I'm not sure what He knew as God but didn't as man. Whatever the case, we know He was asleep in the boat during a life-threatening storm—either because as God, He knew the storm was coming but would not overtake them, or as man He rested in His heavenly Father confident He would see them through—or perhaps a combination of both.

In both instances, Christ modeled for us what it means to "rest" in the Lord. As man, He rested in His Father. As God, He knows what's going on and we can rest in Him. He is sovereign, so we can rest in where He is leading.

Who is the leader of my life? If Christ is the real Leader of my life, then I have to believe that He has led me to where I am right now. If I am not where He wants me to be, then somewhere along the way He ceased to be my Leader. If I am not where He wants me to be, then I need to move. I need to repent and realign myself with His plans and purposes. God will use storms to get us back to where He wants us to be in Him.

If Christ is my Leader, then where I am is where He's

led me, no matter how great the storm. If I believe he is Sovereign God, then I can trust Him because He takes any storm and works it to my greatest good and His greatest glory. I can rest in Him.

Resist expecting the worst. "A furious squall came up, and the waves broke over the boat, so that it was nearly swamped. Jesus was in the stern, sleeping on a cushion. The disciples woke him and said to him, 'Teacher, don't you care if we drown?'" (vv. 37-38).

Were they taking on water? Yes. Was it looking bleak? Absolutely. But were they drowning? No. The disciples didn't wake Christ and say, "Hey, we are taking on water!" They said, "Hey, we are drowning!"

We tend to expect the worst in adversity. Here's a news flash for all of us: The worst may not happen. And if it does, we can rest in the One who is leading.

I heard the story of an elderly woman who lived in London, England, during the bombing in World War II. The possibility of such an attack was imminent, so her adult children attempted to convince her to stay with them outside the London area but she refused. She pointed to a plaque hanging on the wall and said, "You see what that says? You know that's what I live by and I'm not leaving." The plaque read, "Don't worry. It may never happen."

Her children reluctantly gave in and left her there. Not too many days later, the city was bombed as they feared. With all communications cut off and no one allowed into the city right away, it was several days before they could find any information about their mother. Finally, they made it to her apartment building only to find her section of the building quite damaged. They feared the worst.

However, when they arrived at their mother's apartment,

she was sitting in her favorite rocking chair, rocking away. They were relieved she was alive and without injury, but highly upset that she had stubbornly remained. They scolded her saying, "Why didn't you listen to us? We told you so!" One of them pointed to her plaque that now hung crooked on the wall and mockingly questioned, "What do you have to say about your 'don't worry' plaque now?"

The mother suddenly jumped up and said, "Oh, I forgot." She ran over to the plaque and turned it over. The other side read, "Don't worry. You can take it."

Try to resist immediately expecting the worst. It may not happen, but if it does, rest in the One who leads.

Realize Who is in your boat. "Who is this? Even the wind and the waves obey him!" (v. 41).

The disciples did not know who they had in their boat or they wouldn't have been so afraid. Christ leading them through the storm showed them more of Him. They came to a greater understanding of the fullness of Christ. Storms in Christ's hands always lead us to more of Him.

Do we know who we have in the boat? Are we getting to know Him, or is He just someone we know about? Why did the winds, water, and rain obey Him? They obeyed because He made them.

Do we know that we have the Maker and Maintainer of everything in our boat? Do we know Him as Father? Do we know Him as Savior? Do we know Him as Comforter? Do we know Him as Lord? Do we know Him as King? Do we know Him as Friend? Do we know Him as Forgiver? Do we know our God? Or has the storm become our God?

Fear is a faith issue, not a storm issue. Fear is a "how big is my God?" issue.

I heard the story of a pastor who was on a plane when

a huge storm broke out in mid-flight. People were scared and crying. The pastor even confessed that he shared the discomfort and fear of all of those around him. The story goes like this:

> As the pastor looked around the plane, he could see that nearly all the passengers were upset and alarmed. Some were praying. The future seemed ominous and many were wondering if they would make it through the storm.
>
> Suddenly, he saw a little girl and apparently the storm meant nothing to her. She had tucked her feet beneath her as she sat on her seat. She was reading a book and everything within her small world was calm and orderly. Sometimes she closed her eyes, then she would read again, then she would straighten her legs. Worry and fear were not in her world. When the plane was being buffeted by the terrible storm, when it lurched this way and that, as it rose and fell with frightening severity, when all the adults were scared half to death, that marvelous child was completely composed and unafraid. He could hardly believe his eyes.
>
> It was not surprising therefore, when the plane finally reached its destination and all the passengers were hurrying to disembark, that the pastor lingered to speak to the girl whom he had watched for such a long time. Having commented about the storm and behavior of the plane, he asked, "Why were you not afraid?"
>
> The little girl promptly replied, "Because my daddy's the pilot and he is taking me home."

Who's our pilot? Christ said, "Let us go over to the other side." Do we trust Him?

CHAPTER FOUR

THE DEPRESSION GAME

Why are you downcast, O my soul? Why so disturbed within me? Put your hope in God, for I will yet praise him, my Savior and my God (Ps. 42:5-6).

A businessman was in a great deal of trouble because his business was failing. He invested everything he had into the business and he owed everyone. He was even contemplating suicide. As a last resort, he went to a pastor and poured out his story. When he had finished, the pastor said, "Here's what I want you to do. Drive down to the beach and place a beach chair and Bible at the water's edge. Sit down in the beach chair and put the Bible in your lap. Open the Bible and let the wind riffle the pages. When the open Bible comes to rest on a page, look down at the page and read the first thing you see. That will be your answer."

A year later the businessman went back to the pastor and brought his wife and children with him. The man was in a new custom-tailored suit, his wife in a mink coat, and the children dressed to the nines. The businessman pulled an envelope stuffed with money out of his pocket and gave it to the pastor as a donation in thanks for his advice.

The pastor recognized the benefactor and was curious. "You did as I suggested?" he asked.

"Absolutely," replied the businessman.

"You went to the beach?"

"Absolutely."

"You sat in a beach chair with the Bible in your lap?"

"Absolutely."

"You let the pages riffle until they stopped?"

"Absolutely."

"And what were the first words you saw?"

"Chapter 11."

DEPRESSION'S CHALLENGE AND COMPLEXITY

Wouldn't it be great if depression could be resolved that easily? Yet, that is usually not the case because depression is a very challenging and complex issue. It can be quite debilitating and very costly.

For instance, according to the Mental Health America website, every year over 19 million Americans of all ages, gender, ethnicity, and race struggle with depression. It costs as much to treat depression each year as it costs to treat heart disease and AIDS. Due to depression, we spend some $43.7 billion per year on work absenteeism and lost productivity.

Depression is also one of the top three reasons employers report problems in their workplace, preceded only by family crisis and stress. The good news is that eighty percent of the people who struggle with depression and seek treatment have great improvement. The bad news is that less than half of those who struggle with depression ever seek treatment.[1]

One of the reasons that depression is so complex and challenging is because there are a number of symptoms associated with it:

- Trouble sleeping or excessive sleeping
- A dramatic change in appetite, often with weight gain or loss
- Fatigue and lack of energy
- Feelings of worthlessness, self-hate, and inappropriate guilt
- Extreme difficulty concentrating
- Agitation, restlessness, and irritability
- Inactivity and withdrawal from usual activities
- Feelings of hopelessness and helplessness
- Recurring thoughts of death or suicide

Low self-esteem, sudden bursts of anger, and lack of pleasure from activities that normally make one happy are also associated with depression.[2]

Adding to depression's complexity is that it is generally ranked in terms of severity—mild, moderate, or major. The difference in the three is based on the number of symptoms one experiences, for how long and to what extent the symptoms negatively affect one's normal daily life. The mildest forms of depression cause the least amount of disruption while moderate forms noticeably interfere with one's daily life. Major depression often severely impedes one's life with crippling despondency and hopelessness.[3]

If that isn't enough complexity and challenge to this issue, it increases when we look at the range of possible causes:

- Family genetics
- Alcohol or drug abuse
- Childhood events such as abuse or neglect
- Chronic stress
- Death of a friend or relative
- Disappointment at home, work, or school
- Medical conditions
- Nutritional deficiencies
- Overly negative thoughts
- Prolonged pain or having a major illness
- Sleeping problems
- Social isolation (common in the elderly)[4]

The treatments can be as varied as the symptoms and causes. Obviously, how one is treated depends on the degree of depression. Treatments can include diet, exercise, and better sleep habits. Getting more involved in activities that make one happy and serving others are other common treatments. Counseling, medication, or combined treatment are sometimes needed.

Another important element in treating depression is the spiritual or faith side of the issue. Recognizing depression's complexity and challenge with its multiple symptoms, levels, causes, and treatments, the purpose of this chapter is to bring Christ into the equation. I believe that for anyone to live free and whole over depression, Christ must be included in any effective treatment plan. He is critical to defeating depression.

NO EXEMPTIONS

With that said, having Christ in one's life doesn't mean a person is exempt from depression. Over the course of history, some well-known people who loved and trusted the Lord suffered, severely at times, with depression.

David Brainerd was a missionary in the eighteenth century to the Native Americans in New England. Over the course of his ministry, he traveled thousands of miles by horseback to preach the message of Christ. Yet, he battled depression nearly his entire short life. In fact, Brainerd came out of a family that struggled with depression and premature death.

Brainerd's parents died before he reached adulthood. Two brothers died at the ages of twenty-three and thirty-two. His sister died at the age of thirty-four. Brainerd himself died from tuberculosis at the age of twenty-nine. Thomas Brainerd, a relative of the Brainerd family, wrote, "In the whole of the Brainerd family for two hundred years there has been a tendency to a morbid depression, akin to hypochondria."[5]

David Brainerd wrote in his journal, "I was, I think from my youth, something sober and inclined rather to melancholy than the other extreme."[6] His depression became so severe at times that he wanted to die.

> I was so overwhelmed with dejection that I knew not how to live: I longed for death exceedingly. My soul was 'sunk in deep waters,' and 'the floods' were ready to 'drown me.' I was so much oppressed that my soul was in a kind of horror.[7]

Brainerd often encountered bitter weather, rugged terrain, miserable sleeping conditions, excessive isolation, and

loneliness in his travels. Many times he went hungry and battled constant physical illness. Given his many trials, losses,
and his family's apparent tendency toward depression, we
can understand Brainerd's struggle.

However, Brainerd didn't allow depression to rob him of
his calling to preach. With the help of the Lord, He fought
through it. God at work in his life was key to winning his
battle. Interestingly, his diary described that his depression
was different before he chose to follow Christ. He wrote
that even though he still struggled with depression after his
conversion, the love of the Lord was like a rock, an excessive love that caught him in his darkest hour.[8]

Charles Haddon Spurgeon was one of the great orators
of the church in England during the 1800s. Prior to the age
of twenty, he preached more than six hundred times. Each
week approximately twenty thousand copies of his sermons were sold and they have been translated into nearly
twenty languages. It takes a sixty-three volume collection
to contain all of Spurgeon's messages, which is the larg-
est collection of books by any one author in the history
of Christianity. Many people refer to his sermons as mas-
terpieces. Along with his sermon writing, Spurgeon also
wrote many hymns.[9]

Yet, Spurgeon suffered with depression. He also suffered
with gout, rheumatism, and Bright's disease (inflammation
of the kidneys). Spurgeon cared for his invalid wife the last
twenty-seven years of his life. During her illness, she seldom
heard him preach. To add insult to injury, Spurgeon was also
the subject of public ridicule and slander throughout much
of his ministry. All of these circumstances could have been
the reasons for his depression. This is how Spurgeon described his depression:

My spirits were sunken so low that I would weep, by the hour, like a child. Yet, I knew not what I wept for. Despondency is not a virtue, but a vice . . . an iron bolt which so mysteriously fastened the door of hope and holds our spirits in a gloomy prison . . .[10]

I'm not an expert on depression nor am I a licensed psychologist or psychiatrist. I have a master's degree in counseling, and in twenty-five years of ministry as a pastor, I have engaged in many hours of counseling with hundreds of people. I've often heard those struggling with depression describe it as "being in an emotional prison." Like Spurgeon, they felt literally incarcerated in their depressed state.

However, we need to see the full disclosure of Spurgeon's description of depression, for he also proclaimed his primary source of deliverance:

Causeless depression cannot be reasoned with, nor can David's harp charm it away with sweet discoursing. As well fight with the mist as with the shapeless, undefinable, yet all-beclouding hopelessness . . . The iron bolt which so mysteriously fastens the door of hope and holds our spirits in gloomy prison needs a heavenly hand to push it back . . . I am sure there is no remedy for it like a holy faith in God.[11]

Like Brainerd, Spurgeon found refuge and relief in God. To Spurgeon, God's "heavenly hand" was present with him and was the primary source of his help.

When Jesus Christ was in the Garden of Gethsemane just hours before His false arrest, He was feeling the weight and pressure of His impending crucifixion. He asked His closest friends and followers to pray with Him, yet they fell asleep.

"My soul is overwhelmed with sorrow to the point of death. Stay here and keep watch with me." Going a little farther, he fell with his face to the ground and prayed, "My Father, if it is possible, may this cup be taken from me. Yet not as I will, but as you will" (Matt. 26:38-39).

One symptom of depression is overwhelming sorrow, which is how Christ described Himself. He was literally saying He was overwhelmingly sorrowful, greatly distressed, and feeling extreme pain, anguish, and grief. Sounds like He was suffering from depressive emotions.

Think about this a moment—we're talking about Christ here. He seemed to be struggling with some form of depression. So much so, it apparently weighed on Him like death. Who can blame Him? He was about to face the most horrific execution anyone could experience while carrying with Him the heaviness and guilt of humanity's sin. Perhaps what burdened Him most was that He knew such a death would separate Him from His Father for a time and the thought of that was too much to bear. Whatever the causes of His sorrowful state, Christ was battling what sounded a great deal like depression.

If Christ struggled with depression, what might that mean for us? What might we expect from time to time? If He wasn't exempt from it, should we expect to be? I do not mean to say that because Christ had a moment of extreme depression, we're all destined to experience depression at some point, nor am I suggesting that Christ's depression excuses us to live depressed and refuse to seek help. However, if we have depression in our lives at times, it should be helpful to know that even Christ had His moments with sorrow.

But what is most important to me is not so much that Christ became depressed, but what He did when He was depressed. Where did Jesus Christ go? Did He crawl into self-pity? Did He just roll over and quit? He went to His heavenly Father.

What's amazing to me was that Christ asked His Father three times to remove the cup of the cross from Him (see Matt. 26:36-45). The first time He prayed, He went back to His disciples and they were asleep. He woke them and asked them to pray with Him. He went back to pray a second time and prayed the same prayer. He returned to His disciples and they were asleep again. He left them a third time and asked God for another way. Yet, each time He prayed for another way, His greatest desire came forth, "Yet not as I will, but as you will."

Christ appeared to be fighting through His depression by going to the only source that could bring Him through, and He was doing it alone. His closest friends couldn't stay awake long enough to pray with Him. Even after expressing His need for their help, they let Him down. Ever felt that pain and disappointment before?

Friends can be a great source of help in times of depression. Having people who love, encourage, and care for us at our low points is a comforting strength. However, they can cause us to become more depressed if they fail to come through for us. No matter how committed our closest friends may be, they will fall short of meeting our needs at times. We need a greater source.

Christ had a greater source—He had His Father regardless of what His friends did or didn't do. He wasn't going to give in to depression. He continued to cry out to His Father for help, strength, and relief. He fought, even if it meant

71

fighting alone. But He ultimately wasn't alone; His Father was there for Him.

Along with all the other effective treatments of depression we might receive, trusting God is essential to battling depression. God supplies something the other treatments don't: His supernatural presence, power and promises. Having faith in Him positions us to experience those qualities regardless of the strength of our depression.

Please don't misunderstand me. I don't mean to trivialize, over-simplify, or hyper-spiritualize this issue by saying that if we'll just have enough faith we'll get over depression immediately. Depression is a complex and challenging condition that is not easily overcome. However, I am suggesting that with God we have a much better possibility of overcoming and dealing with depression than without Him. Christ, Brainerd, and Spurgeon bear witness to that reality.

So what do we do? How do we trust God in depression? How do we win at the depression game?

PSALM 42

A great way to turn to God in a time of need like depression is to look at the Psalms. The writers of the Psalms were often perplexed, distraught, angry, frightened, and depressed. I enjoy reading these writings, especially when I'm down because the psalmists are so real in their emotions. They cry out of their pain and anguish, often wondering where God is and why He's allowed their plight. They don't hold back any punches with God—they get honest with Him. And, He lets them.

One of my favorite psalms, especially when I'm depressed, is Psalm 42. We aren't completely sure as to the circumstances surrounding the psalmist, but they seem to have him in a depressed state. Yet, in the midst of all his lamenting, he finds solace in God. The psalmist eventually leads us to our ultimate source of hope. Let's first walk through the psalm and get a picture of what the psalmist was facing: "As the deer pants for streams of water, so my soul pants for you, O God. My soul thirsts for God, for the living God. When can I go and meet with God?" (vv. 1-2).

The psalmist describes a deer that has been in a dry place for a very long time without any water. Possibly, he is talking about a deer that has been pursued by predators and has been running for its life. The deer was desperate and could go no farther due to thirst and exhaustion.

People who battle depression sometimes feel like somebody is chasing them. They feel pursued and pressured, having no time to rest or recoup. They're worn out emotionally and need refreshing.

But the psalmist states plainly who he's thirsting for—God. He's not looking or settling for just anything to satisfy his dried up soul. He knows only God will bring the complete relief he seeks and needs. He's depleted and needs God, but he can't find Him. "My tears have been my food day and night, while men say to me all day long, 'Where is your God?'" (v. 3).

Have you ever cried so much that it seems that's all you do anymore? Your emotions seem to be on the surface constantly and you just feel out of control? Remember Spurgeon said that in his depression, he sometimes found himself crying and didn't know why. Perhaps your tears have been your food day and night recently.

Then there's the looming question, "Where are you God?" We can't seem to find Him. As difficult as that is, the real danger comes when those we've been trying to convince of God's reality begin taunting us with our own belief in His existence. They use our depression as a reason to believe God isn't around. Then we feel even more depressed because we now feel as though we're failing God and causing someone else not to believe. Could it get any worse?

> These things I remember as I pour out my soul: how I used to go with the multitude, leading the procession to the house of God, with shouts of joy and thanksgiving among the festive throng (v. 4).

Ever wanted to get back to yesterday? Ever wanted to turn back the clock to a better time? The psalmist is remembering a better time in his life—a time when there was joy. He's remembering when the presence of God was very present and real. Depression can have us longing for yesterday—a better day.

> I say to God my Rock, "Why have you forgotten me? Why must I go about mourning, oppressed by the enemy?" My bones suffer mortal agony as my foes taunt me, saying to me all day long, "Where is your God?" (vv. 9-10).

If we feel God's forgotten us but that our enemy hasn't, then that is often a strong sign that the prison bars of depression are closing in tighter. Most likely, the psalmist was describing a physical foe that was taunting him, but that physical foe represents a spiritual enemy of God and His people. Scripture calls him Satan.

Jesus described Satan, our enemy, as a "thief" that comes only to "steal and kill and destroy," but Christ said not to worry because He had come that we may have life "and have it to the full" (John 10:10). Peter instructed us: "Be self-controlled and alert. Your Enemy the devil prowls around like a roaring lion looking for someone to devour. Resist him, standing firm in the faith" (1 Peter 5:8-9). We're warned to be aware of the Enemy and his schemes, not to be afraid of him. We're also instructed to resist him by standing firm in the truth that life is found and the Enemy defeated in Jesus Christ.

With whatever degree of depression we might struggle, be aware that there is an Enemy who will attempt to weaken our faith with the taunting question, "Where is your God?" He'll whisper thoughts like, "I thought this God of yours was your deliverer—that He would really free you. If you really knew Him, you wouldn't have these feelings. Where is He? See, He's lied to you—He's not there for you." We must realize the source of such thoughts and know they are lies we don't have to buy into and can ultimately defeat. Remember they're false and that soon, God's truth will prevail.

"WHY ARE YOU DOWNCAST?"

In Psalm 42, the psalmist described what he had been going through. He couldn't seem to find God. He felt pressed and pursued. He believed God had forgotten him and his enemies constantly reminded him of his sorrow. He wished he could turn back to a better day but all he could do was weep. He was depressed.

> Why are you downcast, O my soul? Why so disturbed within me? Put your hope in God, for I will yet praise him, my Savior and my God . . . Why are you downcast, O my soul? Why so disturbed within me? Put your hope in God, for I will yet praise him, my Savior and my God (vv. 5-6, 11).

In two places, verses five and eleven, the psalmist revealed the extent of his depression. He used the words "downcast" and "disturbed." In Hebrew, the word *downcast* means "to disintegrate away to dust."[12] Wow—that's depressed! He felt that he was internally disintegrating away to nothing.

The word *disturbed* means "noisy commotion, turmoil and confusion."[13] It's like the clattering sound an armful of pots and pans make when they're dropped on a kitchen floor. This was what the insides of the psalmist were like— an unnerving clatter of confusion and commotion.

We can be grateful for the psalmist's honesty about his feelings. It helps me see that I'm not alone when I encounter similar thoughts, emotions and circumstances. I know that someone else has been there. But here's what helps me most—he didn't stay there. As grateful as I am for the emotional transparency of the psalmist, I am even more grateful that he didn't just tell me how he felt. He told me where he went to deal with his depressed condition.

"Put your hope in God, for I will yet praise him, my Savior and my God."

"PUT YOUR HOPE IN GOD"

The psalmist made an internal decision. After processing his feelings, he faced a choice between justifying his depression based on his circumstances or choosing a better way. It's like he grabbed his own mind and soul by the lapels and said, *Okay, we know we are depressed and it's not good. And regardless of why we're here, we aren't staying here. So, here's what we're going to do! We're going to put our hope in God!*

The word *hope* in the Hebrew means "to wait upon with an attitude of expectation and anticipation."[14] To hope in

God means more than to just passively sit patiently; it means to believe for and anticipate a favorable outcome. The psalmist was waiting on God with the anticipation and expectation that God would somehow someway see him through. Isaiah 40:31 expresses the idea best: "Those who hope in the Lord will renew their strength. They will soar on wings like eagles; they will run and not grow weary, they will walk and not be faint."

But like the psalmist, I must make a decision that I'm not going to put my hope in my emotional condition or my surrounding circumstances, but in the Lord. It's a decision to fight rather than curl up in the corner.

Jesus Christ made the decision to fight when He prayed three different times for His Father's will to be done despite His overwhelming sorrow. David Brainerd fought by residing in Christ's love, while Charles Spurgeon did so by choosing to have an unwavering faith in the hand of God. They all waited with an anticipation and expectation of a favorable outcome.

What is my hope in? Have I had that meeting with my mind to make the internal decision that God will be my ultimate hope? Diet, exercise, fun activities, friends, serving others, counseling, and medication may help a great deal with overcoming depression. Even though the Lord may choose to use some or all of these treatments to heal us, our greatest source of hope is in Him. A resource of strength and power in the Lord remains available to us when other treatments seem to be waning.

"I WILL YET PRAISE HIM"

The psalmist made an external declaration. We immediately see the evidence of the psalmist's decision to hope in the

Lord by his declaration of praise to the Lord. A way we hope in Him is to praise Him.

The word *praise* means "to give thanks through worship." But it also means "to confess, to speak out, and to declare."[15] When we praise God, we thank Him for who He is and what He's done. We also confess and declare His greatness. We speak out the truth of God's character and nature to ourselves, others, our circumstances, and the enemy. We reinforce our decision to hope in Him by declaring in whom we're choosing to place our belief.

Where do we find out who He is and what He promises? The Bible reveals God to us. From His Word, we make our declarations and confessions. We praise Him according to who He's revealed himself to be and according to the promises He's made to us.

We need to look no farther than another psalm, Psalm 119, to connect praising and confessing God even in depressive circumstances. Psalm 119 is primarily a collection of prayers and meditations on the Word of God. This 176-verse psalm is all about the purpose and power of God's Word and the significance of knowing and confessing it.

Here is a selection of verses from Psalm 119 that speak of offering praise, making confession, and having hope even in depressive conditions:

"I will praise you with an upright heart as I learn your righteous laws" (v. 7).

"Praise be to you, O Lord; teach me your decrees. With my lips I recount all the laws that come from your mouth" (vv. 12-13).

"I am laid low in the dust; preserve my life according to your word" (v. 25).

"My soul is weary with sorrow; strengthen me according to your word" (v. 28).

"May your unfailing love come to me, O Lord, your salvation according to your promise; then I will answer the one who taunts me, for I trust in your word. Do not snatch the word of truth from my mouth, for I have put my hope in your laws" (vv. 41-43).

"Though the arrogant have smeared me with lies, I keep your precepts with all my heart. Their hearts are callous and unfeeling, but I delight in your law. It was good for me to be afflicted so that I might learn your decrees" (vv. 69-71).

"My soul faints with longing for your salvation, but I have put my hope in your word. My eyes fail, looking for your promise; I say, 'When will you comfort me?' Though I am like a wineskin in the smoke, I do not forget your decrees" (vv. 81-83).

"Accept, O Lord, the willing praise of my mouth, and teach me your laws. Though I constantly take my life in my hands, I will not forget your law. The wicked have set a snare for me, but I have not strayed from your precepts" (vv. 108-110).

"May my lips overflow with praise, for you teach me your decrees. May my tongue sing of your word, for all your commands are righteous. May your hand be ready to help me, for I have chosen your precepts. I long for your salvation, O Lord, and your law is my delight. Let me live that I may praise you, and may your laws sustain me" (vv. 171-175).

When my second cousin, Chad, was about six years old, he and his family were having dinner with us. Chad was a Nintendo lover and was good at it. He and his four-year-old brother, Jordan, were in the game room playing Nintendo.

While Chad was playing, Jordan became impatient and

wanted a turn. Jordan told Chad to quit and let him play, but Chad ignored him and kept playing. Jordan became more agitated and tried to take the remote from Chad's hand, but Chad dodged him and without hesitating kept on playing. Jordan then began hitting Chad on the arm, but Chad wouldn't quit or defend himself from Jordan's punches. He continued to play while Jordan screamed at him and hit him. Chad began crying, but didn't stop playing.

Finally, Chad had enough and stood up. With tears running down his face and the remote firmly secured in his hand, he looked at his little brother and declared, "I am a Nintendo player! It is who I am! It is what I do!" Chad then sat down and resumed playing. Jordan was in such shock he just gave up.

Perhaps Chad needed a lesson in sharing, but one has to admire and appreciate his passion. He knew who he was and he declared it. He wasn't going to let any attack rob him of it. He made a decision to fight, demonstrated by a declaration of praise.

When depression is pounding us and we find ourselves in tears, let's stand up, hold to God's Word, and declare who He is in us and who we are in Him. Let's demonstrate our decision to place our hope in God by confessing His Word through praise. I believe that, like Jordan, "depression" will be in such shock it will give up.

"MY SAVIOR AND MY GOD"

The psalmist was eternally dependent. God was the psalmist's Savior. The psalmist was a Jew who would have heard God referred to all of his life as the God of Abraham, Isaac, and Jacob. He would have heard the stories of God intervening, leading, and actively working in the lives of his forefathers.

But eventually, this God had to become the psalmist's God. He had to personally believe in his family's God at some point.

I'm a fourth-generation minister. My great-grandmother was a minister to the Native Americans of North Dakota. Both my grandfathers were pastors. My dad is a pastor and I have three uncles who are ministers. Growing up, I heard about the God of my great-grandmother, grandfathers, and parents. I'm grateful for my heritage and the values such a heritage has provided me.

However, I couldn't know God until the God of my forefathers became my God. For the eternal promises and power of God to become active in my life, He had to become *my* Savior. The psalmist didn't say, "I will yet praise him, the God of Abraham, Isaac, and Jacob." He said, "I will yet praise him, my Savior and my God" (Ps. 42:5).

The word *savior*, in Hebrew, means "saving helper; deliverer; and rescuer."[16] God is all that to us in Christ. He is the Savior, which means that although I may be struggling with something like depression right now, there is coming a time when I will never struggle with depression again. The Book of Revelation describes the scene of heaven that is promised to all who trust Christ as their Savior:

> Now the dwelling of God is with men, and he will live with them. They will be his people, and God himself will be with them and be their God. He will wipe every tear from their eyes. There will be no more death or mourning or crying or pain (21:3-4).

In Christ, depression is temporary. Eternal life without depression is forever. God, through Jesus Christ, is the ultimate Rescuer and Deliverer.

I mentioned earlier that my grandfathers were ministers. Both were pioneers, starting close to eighty churches between them in their ministerial careers. My paternal Grandfather Walker was returning home to Beckley, West Virginia early one morning from an out-of-town church meeting. It was dark, rainy, and foggy as he traveled on a curvy mountain road. A train was parked at the railroad crossing, but it could not be seen as he rounded the corner because the crossing signal light was out. The motionless train blended into the darkness of the mountains behind it. By the time my grandfather saw the parked train, he couldn't stop. He hit the train broadside.

The wreck broke his breastbone and shattered his right knee joint. His kneecap was completely destroyed and had to be removed. He suffered an injury to the left side of his head that caused it to swell twice its normal size. He had massive cuts, bruises, and internal bleeding. Blood flowed from his mouth.

At the scene of the accident, railroad workers feared that my grandfather would drown in his own blood, so they sat him up on a bench while they waited for the emergency team to arrive. In his book, *Paths of a Pioneer*, my grandfather described what took place while they waited:

> While I was sitting on the bench in the rain waiting for the ambulance . . . I prayed and told the Lord I was ready to go, but that I had preached the gospel for Him over thirty years and that I would like to live and raise my family if He would let me. Just then a bright and glorious light came, the same in appearance that I had seen at my conversion, only much larger. A great warmth of consolation came over me and I had the assurance that my life would be spared."[17]

When my grandmother and Dad, who was then 18 years old, were finally able to see my grandfather at the hospital in Beckley, they walked into his room and saw him bandaged literally from head-to-toe.

My grandmother, Margaret, walked over to my grandfather and said, "Paul, how are you feeling?"

He responded, "Margaret, I feel great pain in my body, but I feel good in my soul."

His life was hanging in the balance, but he believed he was going to be okay. He had an eternal dependence upon his Savior that whether he lived or died, he was ready. He was at peace because he had a Savior in whom to place his hope.

My grandfather spent forty-eight days in the hospital. Although he eventually recovered from his many injuries, he always walked with a limp. He continued to preach for many years after his accident—limp and all. I heard him say on occasions, "I am limping here today, but there is coming a day when I'll never limp again." It was temporary because he had a Savior.

The limp of depression is painful and may linger with all of us in some form this side of heaven. But it is temporary. God's ultimate, healing relief is eternal. So, when you and I are in our place of depression, let's demonstrate our eternal dependence on our Savior by making the decision to fight depression through hope in Him and to demonstrate that hope by praising Him in open confession and declaration. We may not see a shaft of light from heaven like my grandfather did, but I believe God's presence will be with us to comfort, encourage, deliver, and set us free.

"Put your hope in God, for I will yet praise him, my Savior and my God."

CHAPTER FIVE

THE
ATTITUDE
GAME

"Where you go I will go, and where you stay I will stay. Your
people will be my people and your God my God. Where you
die I will die, and there I will be buried" (Ruth 1:16-17).
"Don't call me Naomi ... Call me Mara [bitter], because the
Almighty has made my life very bitter" (v. 20).

There were two brothers. One was the eternal optimist and the other the eternal pessimist. The pessimist always found something wrong and the optimist always found something right no matter what.

Their parents became quite concerned for both of them and decided to take drastic measures. One night while the boys were sleeping in their separate rooms, the parents went into the pessimistic son's room and filled it to the ceiling with all kinds of gifts they knew their son would love. They knew he wouldn't be able to find anything wrong with such presents. Believing there was no way he could find anything good about a half-filled room of horse manure, the parents filled the optimistic son's room waist deep.

The next morning the parents were sitting at the breakfast table waiting for their sons to emerge from their rooms, fully believing they had solved the problem. The pessimistic son came out first and he was crying his eyes out.

They asked, "What's wrong?"

He replied, "Did you see all those gifts in my room?"

To which they responded, "Yes."

He cried, "Somebody has made a mistake and given me gifts for another boy."

"No, they're for you," his parents assured him.

This didn't help because the son said, "Well, if they are for me, I bet they are all broken or they won't work right."

He was bawling and his parents were stunned. About that time, here came the optimistic son with a shovel in his hand and wearing waders and gloves. He was covered in manure.

He declared, "Isn't it wonderful? Someone has given me a pony and I am going to keep digging until I find him."

In this fictitious story, what was the major difference between the two brothers? It was their *attitude*. One only saw the negative side of life and the other only saw the positive. Although both extremes can prove unhealthy, I believe it's well understood that our attitude can make or break us.

Attitude is simply defined as "one's personal view of something." Attitude is usually a reflection of a person's general outlook on life. One might even call attitude a *worldview*—how someone interprets, responds to, and approaches life. When you get right down to it, attitude is how we *choose* to view, approach, and interpret life. Attitude is a product of our thinking.

Henry Ford said, "Whether you think you can or think you can't . . . you're right."[1] In their book *212: The Extra Degree*, Sam Parker and Mac Anderson echoed Ford's idea, "The only thing that stands between a person and what they want in life is the will to try it and the faith to believe it possible."[2] Charles Swindoll wrote something very similar about attitude in his book *Strengthening Your Grip*:

> The longer I live the more convinced I become that life is 10 percent what happens to us and 90 percent how we respond to it . . . I believe the single most significant decision I can make on a day-to-day basis is my choice of attitude. It is more important than my past, my education, my bankroll, my successes and failures, fame or pain, what other people think of me or say about me, my circumstances, or my position. Attitude is that "single string" that keeps me going or cripples my progress. It alone fuels my fire or assaults my hope. When my attitudes are right, there's no barrier too high, no valley too deep, no dream too extreme, no challenge too great for me.[3]

The Bible states it simply, "As water reflects a face, so a man's heart reflects the man" (Prov. 27:19). In other words, whatever we choose to think about ourselves, others, God, problems, hurt, morality, money—life—will be seen in our attitude. Our attitude is our choice. It's the attitude game.

THAT HURTS, I DON'T CARE WHO YOU ARE

The Book of Ruth is one of the shortest books in the Bible, consisting of only four chapters. Ruth's story is one of human love, tragedy, determination, devotion, friendship, loss, divine redemption, recovery, and renewal. But Ruth is also a story about attitude.

In Ruth 1, we see two attitudes forming in the main characters, Ruth and Naomi. Naomi is a Hebrew woman who was married and had two grown sons. She and her family lived in Bethlehem. A famine struck the area, so they relocated to the land called Moab, which was just east of Bethlehem across the Jordan River in Gentile country. While living there, Naomi's two sons married Moabite women, one who was named Ruth. Later, Naomi's husband and both of her sons died. Naomi decided to return to Bethlehem since there was nothing to really keep her in Moab.

Both of Naomi's daughters-in-law, Ruth and Orpah, wanted to go with her to Bethlehem, but she attempted to convince them to stay. Naomi was trying to get them to see that they still had lives to live. She concluded her urging with, "It is more bitter for me than for you, because the Lord's hand has gone out against me!" (v. 13).

Weeping and sorrowful, Orpah kissed her mother-in-law goodbye and returned to her people. But Ruth wouldn't let Naomi go. She refused to leave:

> "Look," said Naomi, "your sister-in-law is going back to her people and her gods. Go back with her." But Ruth replied, "Don't urge me to leave you or turn back from you. Where you go I will go, and where you stay I will stay. Your people will be my people and your God my God. Where you die I will die, and there I will be buried. May the Lord deal with me, be it ever so severely, if anything but death separates you and me." When Naomi realized that Ruth was determined to go with her, she stopped urging her. So the two

women went on until they came to Bethlehem. When they arrived in Bethlehem the whole town was stirred because of them, and the women exclaimed, "Can this be Naomi?" "Don't call me Naomi," she told them. "Call me Mara because the Almighty has made my life very bitter. I went away full, but the Lord has brought me back empty. Why call me Naomi? The Lord has afflicted me; the Almighty has brought misfortune upon me" (vv. 15-21).

In this touching and heart-breaking portion of the story, we see two women of two very different cultures and worldviews sharing the same painful experience, yet responding with two different attitudes. Ruth was a Gentile, whereas Naomi was a Hebrew. Ruth was a pagan raised under a polytheistic influence, while Naomi was a monotheistic Jew. As different as they were culturally, they shared something common to all—painful suffering. Naomi lost her husband and two boys. Ruth lost her husband. Their loss tied them together.

The suffering of pain and loss is transcultural. Regardless of our upbringing, background, beliefs, race, ethnicity, or socioeconomic status, we all share an unfortunate commonality—pain. We all know hurt. Just watch the news—it reports pain worldwide everyday. Pain ties us all together.

You may recall the story I shared with you in the first chapter about my mission trip to South Africa where my wife and I encountered the lion, Zero. On that same trip, we met Pastor Pasha, a South African who lived in one of the most poverty-stricken areas of South Africa. Our church had helped him plant his church by constructing a one-room church building where his small congregation could meet. He was grateful when Udella and I met him.

His smile was huge, and he couldn't hug us and say "thank you" enough.

Pastor Pasha's excitement about how the building would help them reach their vision was off-the-chart. With joyous exhilaration, he shared some of his current and future plans. He couldn't talk fast enough. His passion was contagious and awe-inspiring.

Yet, in the course of our conversation, he proceeded to tell us of the recent deaths of two of his three sons. They occurred within four weeks of each other. The first son, only twenty-three years old, was murdered in his apartment during an attempted burglary. Four weeks later, his nineteen-year-old son died in an automobile accident. Pastor Pasha performed both his sons' funerals. As he shared his horrible loss with us, we watched the excitement, joy, and passion he displayed earlier give way to hurt, sorrow, and loss. Tears filled his eyes as he described his children. Like any loving parent, he ached for his sons—pain.

Although I couldn't relate to the pain of losing children, I could relate to the pain of loss. I mentioned that I lost my brother to an automobile accident two days after Thanksgiving in 1980. Paul was my only sibling. I was twenty-one at the time and he was only twenty-four. A man driving under the influence on the wrong side of the Interstate struck my brother's car head-on, killing him instantly. As you can imagine, my family was devastated. The pain of loss was incredible. As I write this (nearly thirty years later), the pain rises up as a lump in my throat and I fight back tears—the same type of painful tears I saw in my South African brother's eyes.

There Pastor Pasha and I stood—a South African and an American; one black, the other white; one poor, the other very rich by local standards; living on opposite sides of the world and by all accounts completely different. Yet, we were connected by pain. Sure, there were other things he and I held in common, but few things connected us closer and faster like the shared pain of loss.

It doesn't matter where we're from or what influences we've had in our lives, we share something in common. All of us have hurtful pain in our lives. Naomi and Ruth, though quite different, had suffered loss. Yet they demonstrated two different attitudes in response to their pain.

This is also what we all share in common—how we choose to respond not just to our pain, but to life in general. Attitude is a choice, and just like opinions, we all have one. Choosing how to respond to life is as universal as experiencing life—everyone does it. So, let's look at what Naomi and Ruth can teach us about attitude.

A TALE OF TWO ATTITUDES

When we left Ruth and Naomi, Ruth was telling Naomi she was returning to Bethlehem with her, never to leave her. Naomi, on the other hand, was attempting to persuade Ruth to return to her own people and let her go. But Ruth won Naomi over and the two women traveled to Bethlehem together. As we'll see, two different attitudes emerge between the two. I observe four aspects of their attitudes that will hopefully help us with our own.

Aspect 1: Ruth expressed her need for God; Naomi blamed God.

Hear Ruth respond to Naomi's pleas for her to stay in Moab, "Your people will be my people and your God my God" (v. 16).

Hear Naomi summarize her plight to her daughters-in-law, "No, my daughters. It is more bitter for me than for you, because the Lord's hand has gone out against me!" (v. 13).

Can you hear the difference in the two attitudes? Ruth expressed her need for God in this situation while Naomi blamed God. What I find interesting is that Ruth most likely learned about God from Naomi and her family. How else would Ruth have known about the God Almighty? Ruth was a Gentile brought up believing in many false gods. Remember that Naomi's other daughter-in-law, Orpah, went back to her people and their foreign gods (v. 15). But Ruth refused and claimed the true God as her own.

Ruth was hurting like Naomi, yet she demonstrated a very different attitude. Ruth knew she needed God. Naomi was mad at God.

A pastor friend of mine, who I'll name Pastor John, told me the story of a woman who called him to express her anger about a decision he had made. Pastor John had asked a staff pastor from another church to come work for him in his church. The staff pastor prayed about it and felt it was of God for him to leave his church to work for my friend. A woman who belonged to the church where the staff pastor was leaving became very hurt and upset to hear that her pastor, whom she greatly admired, was going to work for someone else. She found Pastor John's number and called him angered over the situation and said, "I hope you grow a big wart on the end of your nose!"

My friend tried to sympathize with her loss and thought he'd be able to ease her pain by helping her see that this was something her former staff pastor believed was of God. So, he replied to her, "Ma'am, I am sorry but it was his decision. He felt it was God, so God is the one who really orchestrated this. We believe this is His will."

There was a moment of silence on the other end of the line and then the woman responded, "Well, I hope God grows a wart on the end of his nose, too!" And then she hung up.

There is scriptural evidence that God understands and is patient with us when we are mad at Him. He demonstrated patience with Naomi. The Psalms are filled with people expressing their anger toward God and God allowing it. My dad shares that after my brother's death, he was able to work through his anger with God by reading the Psalms. Another great read that reveals God's patience and understanding with us in our anger is Job. Check out Job's story and you'll enjoy some candid and intense conversations between Job and God. And Job lived to tell the tale.

However, if we read such biblical sources we'll soon see that although we can be angry with God, we can't stay angry with Him. We can be mad at Him but we don't need to stay mad at Him. At some point if we want to move past the pain of loss, our anger with Him will have to shift to a need for Him. Otherwise, we'll remain in the pain and our anger can easily turn to bitterness. Job and the psalmists eventually shifted their anger with God to an honest cry of their need for Him.

I mentioned my dad reading through the Psalms to help him move through his anger. He further shares that they helped him get honest with God about his feelings. Dad poured out his heart and soul to God. He couldn't just hold it in—he had to express it—and so do we. We can't just blame God; we have to talk to Him. We can't give Him the silent treatment because it only hurts us.

Dad also said that he had to do more than express his feelings to God; he had to listen to Him. When he would pour out his anger, Dad couldn't just walk away. He had to wait to hear God. Some ways that Dad heard God was through

God's Word, through his thoughts, through worship, and through the stories of others who had walked in his shoes. But Dad had to be willing to listen. Whatever ways God chooses to speak to us, we must be open to hearing Him.

So, are we listening to Him? Are we speaking to Him? Being willing to cry out to God and to hear Him is a clear sign that we are moving from blaming Him to needing Him. It's okay to be angry with God. But there comes a point and time when we all have to say, "Regardless of what I am feeling about You, God, I need You." It's in the attitude of needing Him, not blaming Him, that we find Him and His strength.

Aspect 2: Ruth declared her identity; Naomi denounced her identity.

Ruth claimed Naomi's people—God's chosen people of Israel—to be her people. She was declaring her identity as one of God's people. She was God's daughter and she wasn't going to say otherwise.

Naomi, on the other hand, denounced her very name. Her name Naomi meant "pleasant." Yet, she didn't want to be called pleasant. She renamed herself, Mara, which meant "bitter." In other words, Naomi was saying, "Don't call me pleasant; call me bitter—that's who I am."

While Naomi denounced who she was in God, Ruth declared the opposite. She was one of God's people now. All Naomi could identify with was her pain and anger. Her loss was becoming her god and determining who she was. Ruth could only express her need for God, which kept her centered in belonging to Him.

What is your identity? What can you stand on that keeps you anchored when your life is going through the worst of times? Who do you belong to, regardless? There is nothing outside of the eternal love of God that can keep us grounded in real hope, purpose, healing, and meaning. Whatever we identify with will ultimately determine our attitude.

My family faced this very challenge when we were dealing with the bitterness, anger, and pain of my brother's death. What has enabled us to move forward in such great loss has been God's help to know who we are in Him. My mom established that we would place our identity in Him as early as my brother's funeral.

The service was over and like all traditional funeral services, the casket was wheeled out with the family following behind. Mom and Dad were first behind the casket and then I followed them. As we were walking out, the choir was singing a song that I will never forget. The chorus said: "Keep on praising Him, keep on praising Him, though you feel there is no way. Praise Him in the cold blackened night. For to praise Him in the darkness brings the light."[4]

As those words echoed throughout the sanctuary, my mom raised her hands in worship to God. She was following the dead body of her first-born child with her hands lifted in praise to her God.

Why? Was she trying to impress the people around her? No, she couldn't have cared less at that moment what people thought. Was it just some religious expression? No, religious expressions alone are meaningless and empty. Mom was declaring who she was and to whom she belonged. She was making it known that although her son had been taken away from her, she was still the daughter of the Most High God. Like Ruth, she was expressing her need for God and declaring Him her source of identity.

Aspect 3: Ruth was other-focused; Naomi was self-focused.

What did we hear Naomi say? "Look what has happened to me." In fact, she told Ruth and Orpah that she had more reason to be bitter than they did (v. 13). It was all about her. She only focused on herself.

What did we hear Ruth say? "Where you die I will die, and there I will be buried. May the Lord deal with me, be it ever so severely, if anything but death separates you and me" (v.17). She pledged lifetime service to Naomi. Ruth was hurting just like Naomi, yet she displayed an attitude that was other-focused. It wasn't just about her. She realized that there was someone else who was in need.

I heard a true story of a woman who was considering joining a particular church and wanted to discuss this with the pastor. Unfortunately, the woman was very negative, divisive, and self-centered and had a track record of causing trouble in several churches.

During her conversation with the pastor, he shared with the woman what he had heard about her. It wasn't easy for her to hear. She became defensive at first, but the pastor remained patient and understanding. Soon, the woman opened up to the pastor about the pain and losses in her life, using them as the reason for her anger and bitterness.

Sympathizing with her hurt, the pastor believed the best help for the woman would be for her to get outside herself and help others. He suggested this to her and asked for her assistance in visiting people in the hospital and nursing homes. She was shocked with the idea at first. Although she wasn't thrilled about it, she gave in to appease the pastor. The pastor provided her with training and soon the woman started her visitation project. Although she initially agreed to humor the pastor, her attitude dramatically changed after several weeks.

She came to realize that there were other people with

problems far greater than hers who demonstrated more positive attitudes. She also witnessed how those she served were blessed because of her care. It changed her life. She eventually joined the church and started a hospital/nursing home ministry that became a strong outreach of that church for many years.

Regardless of our life-condition, there are people within our sphere of influence that we can serve. We just need an other-centered attitude. Not only will this change our lives, we will see positive changes in other people's lives as a direct result of our willingness to become less self-focused.

Aspect 4: Ruth was motivated by a divine purpose; Naomi by a depressed pity.

Ruth seemed to believe that God's purpose for her was to serve Naomi. "May the Lord deal with me, be it ever so severely, if anything but death separates you and me" (v. 17). Ruth was so sold on her divine purpose that she was willing to undergo severe judgment should she ever abandon it. The pain of her loss didn't steal her desire for God's purpose.

Naomi appeared to lose her sense of divine purpose. When she returned to Bethlehem, she said the reason for her bitterness was that she went away full but the Lord brought her back empty (v. 21). In other words, when Naomi left Bethlehem, she was filled with the purpose of being a wife and mother. Now with her husband and sons dead, she saw no useful purpose. As far as she was concerned, her life was over. She was sinking into an attitude of self-pity as her pain robbed her purpose.

The Book of Romans offers an amazing truth and promise about purpose: "And we know that in all things God works for the good of those who love him, who have been

97

called according to his purpose" (8:28). God is not an un-involved bystander in our lives, but the sovereign God who is at work to bring out His purpose. The promise doesn't say all that happens to us is good, but that God is at work in all of it to bring about the best outcome. But the clincher is that we have to want His purpose. This promise is for those "called according to his purpose."

Those called according to God's purpose are those who trust that God is at work on their behalf even when they don't see Him clearly. They show their trust by consistently aligning their lives with His promises and commands al-though their present circumstances may be bad. They fight self-pity and display the type of attitude shown by Job. Even when he thought God was the one afflicting him, he said, "Though he slay me, yet will I hope in him" (Job 13:15). If anyone had a right to self-pity, it was Job. And he definitely had bouts of self-pity, but he battled it. He kept hoping in God, believing his divine purpose was at work.

I'm reminded of people of my generation that display Ruth and Job-like attitudes. People like Joni Eareckson Tada who, as a teenage girl, suffered a diving accident causing a spinal injury that left her a wheelchair-bound quadriplegic. She is now an amazing author, artist (she paints by using a paintbrush held with her teeth), and speaker used of God to start a worldwide organization dedicated to helping the disability community. Untold numbers of families around the world have been helped through her ministry.[5]

I think of someone like Dave Roever who, while serving in combat in Vietnam, had a phosphorous grenade blow up in his hand burning his body beyond recognition. He spent fourteen months in the hospital undergoing multiple major surgeries. Today, still badly scarred, Roever has been used by God to travel the globe speaking in public schools, military installations, conventions, churches and even appearing on television telling millions of people about hope and faith in God. He's also established charitable organizations designed to reach out to the military wounded and their families.[6]

David Ring, who was born with Cerebral Palsy leaving him with a severe speech impediment and poor motor skills, is another person that comes to mind. He was orphaned at the age of fourteen and because no one wanted him, he was passed from family to family as he grew up never having a place to call home. He suffered constant physical pain, public ridicule, and overwhelming discouragement. Yet, through all of this, God has used him as an author and speaker inspiring people everywhere to never give up on God. His opening line is, "I have Cerebral Palsy—what's your problem?"[7]

By their own admission in writing and public appearances, all three struggled with self-pity. But the key word here is "struggled." They fought it. They didn't give in to it. They trusted that God had a plan and purpose at work. Their motivation was to know, live by, and live out that purpose.

Is that easy? No.

Does it take work? Yes.

Is it worth it? Absolutely!

How do we develop that kind of attitude? Try Ruth. She expressed her need for God, declared her identity in Him, and was other-centered. I believe if we'll do the same, we'll discover and live by God's divine and sovereign purposes. And guess what else? We'll experience God's healing and wholeness in the process.

You have to read the rest of the Ruth story because Naomi doesn't stay in her grief-stricken state. God brings her out in a big way. He does some amazing stuff in, through, and for Ruth and Naomi. It's a great read (and it's short).

"THE FIRST ORDER OF BUSINESS"

When I was a pastor in Orlando, Florida, we had an extensive food pantry ministry. Many people participated in keeping it stocked and helping us distribute food to the homeless. But there was one gentleman who every month did one of two things: he would either give us a check for three hundred dollars to stock the pantry or he would personally go out and spend that amount on groceries and bring them to the pantry. He was passionately dedicated.

He was an elderly man and unfortunately developed cancer, which prohibited him from physically buying and delivering the groceries for the pantry. But he faithfully provided a check every month so we could stock it. He was like clock work. You could count on that check regardless. Soon he was totally bed-ridden and was eventually placed in the hospital.

One day I received a phone call from his daughter asking me to visit because they weren't sure how much longer he'd be with us. Accompanied by one of our elders who knew this gentleman well, I went to visit. Surprisingly, he was quite alert for someone in his condition. After we talked awhile, he said, "Pastor, I really love to hear you sing choruses and I would like to sing some worship choruses."

I said, "Okay, what's one of your favorites?"

He said, "'Surely the Presence.'" So we sang it.

Though the elder with me didn't sing very well, he felt compelled to sing along. He and I together did not make a good duet. Knowing this, I don't know what possessed me

100

to do what I did next. When we finished the chorus, I asked the man if he had another one he'd like to sing. What was I thinking? The man said, "Yes, 'Standing on Holy Ground.'" So we sang it and it was worse.

I didn't ask for another request. I didn't have to because the man began to sing on his own without the elder and me. I guess we were so bad he thought he'd rescue us. He sang the old hymn, "He touched me, He touched me, and oh the joy that floods my soul. Something happened and now I know He touched me and made me whole." While I was caught up in my own worry about how we sounded, I finally noticed that the man was worshiping God. Our sound wasn't an issue for him because it wasn't about us; it was about God.

There I stood as a young pastor trying to find the words to comfort a dying man and the dying man was not only comforting me but also teaching me. You talk about an attitude of expressing your need for God, declaring your identity in Him, and serving others—this guy was amazing.

Two days later the man died and went to be with the Lord. His daughter came to my office shortly thereafter to make the funeral arrangements. She walked into my office and after taking a seat, she said, "Here is the first order of business, Pastor. My dad's last act before he died was asking me to write a check for him to give to the church to fill the food pantry. Here it is." She handed me a check for four hundred dollars.

Nothing can rob us of an attitude motivated by divine purpose if we won't let it. The power of God is greater than any amount of pain of loss. Is He our need? Is He our identity? Are we available for His use to serve others?

The choice is ours.

LET THE GAMES END...

Games are fun, except when we're playing them in our minds. Just as we place our entertaining games back in the box when they're over, we have to rid our minds of thinking that impairs healthy living. *Mind Games* has attempted to reveal ways to overcome crippling thoughts that attempt to control our lives. Let's quickly recap what we've looked at together.

Our belief about a situation ultimately determines our response to it. We can't just blame the circumstance for how we feel or act; we have to take responsibility for our response choices. To ensure our beliefs are built on a firm foundation of truth, we need to look to God's Word and allow the Holy Spirit to replace our faulty beliefs with God's transforming truth. It's the belief game.

We learned the secret to real contentment—Jesus Christ. He's the eternal vertical life-source that enables us to experience lasting contentment regardless of circumstances. Our tendency, however, is to live and measure life by the horizontal sources of "who others are" and "what others have." These produce unhealthy discontentment that leaves us constantly lacking and looking for more. The discontentment game is learning to shift our need for identity, purpose, and security from the limited temporary sources of the horizontal life to the eternal, unlimited, and ever-increasing vertical life found in Christ.

We also discovered together that the size of our fear isn't the result of the size of our storm but the size of our faith. Fear is a faith issue. The fear game calls for us to have faith in someone who is greater than our storm and secures our eternal destiny. Overcoming unhealthy fear is possible if we'll entrust the leadership of our lives to our Maker, resting in Him to supply us with His abundant living even when we're overwhelmed by life's unexpected winds and waves.

Depression is a complex and challenging condition of life to which we're all susceptible. No one is exempt from depression's touch—even Jesus Christ experienced some depression. Depression has many symptoms and is treated in a variety of ways. Yet, essential to any treatment plan is reliance on God. The depression game is deciding to fight depression's darkness with God's presence, power, and promises. It's choosing to hope in Him, declare His truths, and completely depend on His unfailing character.

The pain of suffering loss is universal but so is the attitude we form in the midst of our pain. Attitude is huge not only in how we heal but in how we live. Attitude can either make or break us. It determines us and is vital to defeating the mind games we can play on ourselves during painful times. The attitude game is deciding to express our need for God more than needing to express our anger at Him; it's deciding to draw our identity from Him instead of allowing our pain to identify us; it's deciding to look beyond ourselves to the needs of others; and it's deciding to live according to God's divine purposes, not according to our immobilizing self-pity.

TWO COMMON THREADS

As we've journeyed through these five mind games together, I trust you've noticed two common threads to overcoming all of them. The first is our God, who through Christ, and by His Spirit and Word, develops sound and healthy minds. He and His ways defeat crippling thoughts and heal wounded minds. God and His truth literally transform our thinking, therefore transforming our lives. With God at work in us, through Christ, and by the Holy Spirit and His Word, there is victory over the futility of hindering mind games.

The second common thread is our choice. There's a tremendous amount of power in choice. We must decide to live in and according to God and His truth—to align our lives and thinking with who He is and what He claims. Joshua states the power of choice quite plainly when he addressed the Israelites just before they were to inhabit the land God promised them. They had a decision to make as to how they were going to think and live.

> Now fear the Lord and serve him with all faithfulness. . . . But if serving the Lord seems undesirable to you, then choose for yourselves this day whom you will serve, whether the gods

105

your forefathers served beyond the River, or the gods of the Amorites, in whose land you are living. But as for me and my household, we will serve the Lord (Josh. 24:14-15).

The gods the Israelites' forefathers served beyond the River and the gods of the Amorites where the Israelites presently lived were false gods. The people had a choice: to live influenced by the dysfunctions formed in their families through following false gods, by the false ideologies of the culture in which they lived, or by the new and living way God gave them. They had to decide, and so do we!

Joshua's challenge rings out to us right now and we must choose. How will we complete the statement, "As for me and my house, we will . . ."? Perhaps another way to state it is, "As for me and my way of thinking, I will . . ." The choice is ours.

The list of mind games we've discussed is not exhaustive by any means. There are many more, I'm sure. But regardless of how many mind games exist, choosing to align with Christ and His claims is the ultimate answer to overcoming them.

So, by the power and authority of Almighty God made available to us through the person and work of Christ, activated within us by the Holy Spirit, join me today in placing the dysfunctional mind games of our past, the false mind games of our culture, and the challenging mind games of our painful circumstances back in the box. Let the crippling mind games end and let the full and free life that is ours in Christ begin!

ENDNOTES

CHAPTER ONE

1. Spiros Zodhiates, ed., *Hebrew Greek Key Word Study Bible, NIV* (Chattanooga: AMG International, 1996), 1651.
2. Ibid., 1676.
3. Ibid.
4. *Encarta,* <http://encarta.msn.com> (29 May 2009).

CHAPTER TWO

1. Gerald F. Hawthorne, *Word Biblical Commentary, Phillipians, Vol. 43* (Waco: Word, 1983), 198.
2. Spiros Zodhiates, ed. *Hebrew Greek Key Word Study Bible, NIV* (Chattanooga: AMG International, 1996), 1926.
3. Phil McHugh, "The Strength of the Lord," Larnelle Harris, River Oaks Music: 1987.

CHAPTER THREE

1. *Encarta,* <http://encarta.msn.com> (29 May 2009).

CHAPTER FOUR

1. *Mental Health America.* <http://www.mentalhealthamerica.net> (29 May 2009).
2. *New York Times.* <http://health.nytimes.com/health/guides/symptoms/depression/overview.html#top> (29 May 2009).
3. *Workingwell.* <http://www.workingwell.org.au/2.html> (29 May 2009).
4. *New York Times.* <http://health.nytimes.com/health/guides/symptoms/depression/overview.html#top> (29 May 2009).
5. John Piper, *Oh, That I May Never Loiter On My Heavenly Journey! Reflections on the Life and Ministry of David Brainerd,* 31 Jan. 1990, http://www.desiringgod.org/ResourceLibrary/Biographies/1461_Oh_That_I_May_Never_Loiter_On_My_Heavenly_Journey/ (29 May 2009).
6. Ibid.
7. Ibid.
8. Ibid.

9. John Piper, *Charles Spurgeon: Preaching Through Adversity, 31 Jan. 1995, http://www.desiringgod.org/ResourceLibrary/Biographies/1469_Charles_Spurgeon_Preaching_Through_Adversity/* (29 May 2009).

10. Ibid.

11. Ibid.

12. Spiros Zodhiates, ed., *Hebrew Greek Key Word Study Bible, NIV* (Chattanooga: AMG International, 1996), 2022.

13. Ibid., 1928.

14. Ibid., 1520

15. Ibid.

16. Ibid., 1522

17. Paul H. Walker, *Paths of a Pioneer* (Cleveland, Tennessee: 1971), 313.

CHAPTER FIVE

1. Sam Parker and Mac Anderson, *212: The Extra Degree* (Aurora: Simple Truths, 2006), 73.

2. Ibid., 53.

3. Charles Swindoll, *Strengthening Your Grip* (Waco: Word Books, 1982), 207.

4. Carolyn Gillman, *Just Keep Praising Him* (Crown-Aztec Music: 1977).

5. Joni Eareckson Tada, <*http://www.joniandfriends.org*> (29 May 2009).

6. Dave Roever, <*http://www.daveroever.org*> (29 May 2009).

7. David Ring, <*http://www.davidring.org*> (29 May 2009).